D1590292

THE
COLLAPSIBLE
MANNEQUIN

CHARLOTTE MATTHEWS

Black Rose Writing | Texas

ISBN: 978-1-68433-607-4
PUBLISHED BY BLACK ROSE WRITING
www.blackrosewriting.com

Printed in the United States of America
Suggested Retail Price (SRP) $18.95

The Collapsible Mannequin is printed in Book Antiqua

*As a planet-friendly publisher, Black Rose Writing does its best to eliminate unnecessary waste to reduce paper usage and energy costs, while never compromising the reading experience. As a result, the final word count vs. page count may not meet common expectations.

To Albert and Emma and Garland

THE
COLLAPSIBLE
MANNEQUIN

There are no photographs of miracles.
—Rebecca Solnit

Here I am shredding The Rolla Daily News at the kitchen table, pasting stories about people, one on top of another. Sometimes the words bleed together, and I imagine strangers meeting. Maybe they will meet in real life, too. Maybe, at this very moment, they are sharing a booth at The Waffle House, drinking hot coffee with steam rising in plumes from heavy, white mugs. I'm making a snowy owl out of papier mâché. When Mr. Abel told us the white plumage helps them hide, I knew this was the bird for me. Plus, their parents keep on taking care of them even after they can fly — for ten weeks. In the life of an owl, that's a good long time.

When Mom wakes up, I am reading an article about the opening day of trout season. It includes a picture of a boy my age dressed in a camo hoodie holding up a fish as big as his head. I'm wondering who took him to the lake and whether he skipped school to go. *Come and see my little man* is what my mother says, her voice sounding strange and far-off.

The only time I'm in Mom's room is when she's not there, so this is different. Next to her bed is a black case the size of a highchair. She tells me to open it, and I am met by a plastic man folded at the waist. He's dressed in a banker's suit, grey with vertical stripes of a darker grey. He even has on shoes, wingtips, quite the fancy getup. I'm sure stranger things have happened, but this one definitely tops my list.

Mom says I can check him out. So, I am kneeling on my mother's bedroom floor touching a man in a box. His skin, if you want to call it that, is cold and hard and unforgiving, his hair stiff as the stems of fallen leaves. Mom is smoking her morning cigarette, occasionally letting it perch on the indent of the yellow, glass ashtray. The ashen part has gotten super long, but I won't point that one out because she is talking in her 'I'm-explaining-important-things voice'. She says the word mannequin comes from the Dutch word manneken, which means little man or figurine. She says she doesn't like the word dummy for mannequin because it passes a judgement where no judgement is needed. Mom's like that, all the time squeezing in little life lessons, hoping they'll seep into me without my say so.

But all I can focus on is her cigarette ash, how it looks like it is getting ready to drop off onto the checkered sheet, make one of those perfect circles with charred edges she hates so much. Then, suddenly, she tells me I can go back to whatever I had been doing. I leave, shut her door carefully behind me the way she does when she checks on me after I'm in bed. I'll remember this for a good long time. It will stick with me the way a burr sticks to your sweater hours after a walk in the woods. It stays with you as your sweater's passenger, your own personal sidekick.

In a year and one month, I will be older than I will be in just one year. In eight years, I will have a completely different life. Ever think about that for yourself? Shocking, really. I need to find out every single thing I can about this foldable man, this little man, this mannequin, who is now apparently living with us. When I Google mannequin, the computer says the first ones were made in France out of papier mâché, exactly what I had been doing before I went into Mom's room. Next, mannequins were of wax, more lifelike. People would stand in front of department store windows to behold a make-believe world frozen in place. The waxen figures would stare out of the plate-glass, unblinking. *Like my owl*, I say to our cat Peaches, *but not like you.*

Peaches and I spend hordes of time together. Because we live next door to the Gateway Rent-to-Own, there's plenty for both of us to watch: dollies with dryers balanced on their ends, La-Z-Boys being stuffed into trucks. It looks, at first, like there's no way they'll fit, but then, lo-and-behold, in goes the brown, oversized chair whose footrest, I know, pops out. I like the way everyone wears gloves, protecting the furniture they need to touch. The best thing, though, is how this one guy, who must be the boss of loading up the trucks, can turn his thumb back on itself. Once he gets the desk or sofa stuffed into the truck's body, he gives a thumbs up to the person on the ramp below, and his finger bends way, way back — like another thirty degrees. Whenever I try, my thumb just sticks straight up in the air. *No thumbend for me*, I say to Peaches.

Peaches sits on the couch's arm, and we look out the front window together. We're watching the world go by. This afternoon it's kids practicing soccer in the empty lot across the street. So, I turn my attention back to Peaches who moves and breathes, unlike Mom's mannequin. Today, I explain to Peaches what makes it possible for birds to perch on power lines without getting electrocuted. She is all the time staring at them, breathes faster and moves her whiskers while doing so—as if afraid for their very lives. I tell her that electricity zipping through a power line will take the path of least resistance, not stopping for anything. But Peaches ignores me. She keeps on gaping at the birds, breathing and looking, looking and breathing. Bird-gaping, I call it.

Even though there's just a small spit of grass outside our apartment, a misshapen but sturdy crabapple tree has stayed alive there. Last spring, Mom hung a bird feeder from a clothes hanger, then hung the hanger on one of the tree's branches, and now birds line up on the wire hanger. It's like they are waiting to get a drink at the water fountain during the break in PE. The only downside is when a car or truck pulls into the parking lot. I feel sorry for the bird about to get his turn when the sound of an engine scares them all off. Whoosh and the birds are gone, just like that. One time an old, blue Chevy with a loud engine circled the parking lot, and the birds were out of there faster than you can say jack rabbit. Last week, a dove just sat on top of the feeder. He or she—I couldn't tell which—perched there, kind of poofed out, probably keeping warm. Because I had the sneaking sensation that Mr. or Mrs. Dove might appreciate a little space, a little privacy, while keeping warm, I tiptoed away from the window.

After this, I Googled doves. Did you know that they build the flimsiest of nests? While most other birds construct sturdy, cozy dwellings for their young, doves just slap it all together like they are in a huge hurry. In some species of birds, the dad is even the one to take care of the babies. And penguins really take the cake. The male penguin stands on the ice keeping the egg warm on top of his feet while the mom penguin goes off gallivanting on her own. She's having the time of her life while the dad stays put, keeps the home fires burning, so to speak.

Our apartment looks more like doves live here because of the way it's just kind of pieced together. I'm pretty sure it used to be a store because it's the exact shape and size of Rent-To-Own. The only difference is ours is where we live and theirs is where they rent things for people to live with. They have three trucks, diesel ones, so we know if anyone's coming or going. The trucks putter loudly once the driver turns the key, and the sound is exactly like Peaches' purring, only amplified a lot.

One brilliant thing about Rent-to-Own is that to the left of where you walk in, there's this glass popcorn popper going pop pop pop pop pop sending out white popcorn for all to behold. Beside it, on a cart, are paper bags with the word *popcorn* written in capital red letters. You are free to help yourself. The first time I went in I was with Mom, and they gave us a personalized tour of the store. They explained how if we put some money down, we could take what we wanted and, one day, it would be our own. It would be ours to keep. Mom made it perfectly clear that we would not rent to own, not now, not ever. The look on her face turned tense when she said it, almost like she was chewing on the words, her mouth real tight. Still, whenever I go in, they tell me it's okay if I lounge in a La-Z-Boy and munch on popcorn in front of the wide screen. *Make yourself at home, buddy,* is what this one guy, Larry, says kind of in the voice of a dad. Sometimes I think about what it would be like to have Larry around the house. I might even get to have my picture in the paper, me holding up an enormous fish on the opening day of trout season.

TAKE A SAD SONG AND MAKE IT BETTER—SARAH

I don't know if I've gotten anything right. As a child, all those long days, I knew too much too soon. That's why I took to writing stories: to make a world I could climb into, a world all my own. Because my mother's constant companions were distrust and resentment, I picked up early on the fact that there was not much room for me in her world. Sometimes, I would try to cheer her up by citing song lyrics, reminding her how those British boys wanted us to *take a sad song and make it better.* But she just scoffed, went back to refolding my socks, one of her many distractions. If you let a truth live inside you for too long, it takes over, precisely the way a virus does. I guess that's what she did, convinced herself that she should be suspicious and that there are no miracles no matter how hard you wish for them.

ACT LIKE YOU DON'T CARE—CLARENCE

Every morning our teacher, Mr. Abel, starts by putting a question of the day on the board. We answer the question on notecards, which we then stuff into a yellow box that looks like it used to hold tissues. The answer box stays on the left front corner of Mr. Abel's desk all day long. Before dismissal, he randomly picks a few of our notecards to read aloud. The brilliant thing is that the questions don't have one right or definite answer. Maybe a better way to put this would be to say that every answer is correct. That means every single answer is equally right. He's asking for our opinion; he's asking what we think. Example: what shape was the first ever snowflake? What is the sweetest flavor of ice cream? Why does the word llama seem so odd when you take time to think about it? Tomorrow I will ask Mr. Abel if he'll use *What does a cat's purring sound like?* as a question. I bet there will be some magnificent ideas, some top-notch answers to that one.

It's my favorite part of school, the question of the day. I love how Mr. Abel pulls the card out of the box slowly, like it is something rare and spectacular we have been waiting our entire lives to see. First, he reads the chosen answer silently to himself, reads it in his own head. I'm guessing he does this to make sure he doesn't make a mistake. Plus, some kids have handwriting that is probably hard for him to read. Next, he clears his throat; he always clears his throat three times, and it sounds like that loud Chevy's engine catching. Finally, he peers up over his glasses to scan the room to make sure we are all attentively listening before he reads the question out loud. After he reads it, we raise our hands and share our own personal answers to the question. Then we go home.

But about a month ago, Mr. Abel put down the card he was about to read. He put it down deliberately, almost with a bit of anger, and told four boys who were sitting on the edge of their seats, saying, *ooh, ooh, pick me, pick me*, that he considered it to be a very serious kind of bullying to copy how someone else acts. He told them that if they did it again, they would find themselves in the principal's office. I knew it was me they were copying because I had — until that day — done precisely what those boys were doing. So, I've learned to act like I don't care all that much when I raise my hand. And I no longer sit on the edge of my seat.

I have set out to memorize an unfamiliar word each week. If you can collect stamps, coins, and seashells, why not collect something that stays with you at all times, something that can walk around with you? People stare at me when I blurt out one of my collected words. I try not to use any collected words on the playground to keep kids from looking at me and saying *Clarence-word*. The only person who seems to really appreciate all the words I've collected is the library checkout lady who grins from ear to ear when I use one. It's like she and I have our own little club, and when I say one of the words it's our secret handshake.

My technique for building my word collection is simple: every Sunday I get out the huge dictionary that Mom calls unabridged, and I close my eyes, flop the book open, put my finger down, and wherever it lands, that's the word of the week, bang, just like that. I write commotion or gargantuan or occurrence or uproarious or meander or stellar or indelible — plus whatever the dictionary says the word means — on a notecard. For the rest of the week, all the way until the following Sunday, that notecard cruises around with me in my pocket. When things get slow, I just whip it out and read it. Usually by the time Wednesday rolls around, the word is mine. It's something I have collected and there is no way to lose it and no way anyone can take it away from me.

I've also figured that if I eat a different brand of breakfast cereal each week, something good is bound to happen. With names like Special K, Smart Start, Lucky Charms, Total, and Life, how can you go wrong? Good odds for happy times, I'd say. So, on Saturday mornings I walk to Kroger with my allowance — five dollars — folded in a triangle in my back left pocket. It's a little under a mile to The Wayside Shopping Center, and I'm allowed to go there by myself as long as I stay facing traffic and on the sidewalk. I used to count my steps, two per square, but one time my left toe ended up on a crack. The entire rest of that day,

I made myself hold my breath one minute each hour in hopes the bad luck might disappear. Since then, I have stopped counting steps. I'm sure you can see why.

At customer service, they give out free balloons, and not only to little kids. All you have to do is ask for one. The woman behind the counter — Sheeree, her name tag says — puts on a pair of plastic safety glasses, then asks you what color you want, blue, orange, green, pink, or white. Next, she fills your chosen balloon with helium. She makes them so full it seems like they will burst. But none ever has. I hold my breath while she's got the balloon hooked onto the helium machine. I tell myself I'm holding good luck to make it so the balloon won't go pop right there in Sheeree's hand.

You might wonder what a twelve-year-old like me is doing with a balloon. Well, after I get home, I head to my room in a beeline so Mom won't see what I have in tow. Then I tie the balloon to my desk chair and walk to the kitchen where she's sitting staring into her coffee mug like something fantastic and unexpected might happen in it, like it's a tv show and she doesn't want to miss out on any of the action. Hoping to make her smile, I sing, *Lucky Charms, they're magically delicious*, as I open up the cabinet above the sink to stash my cereal away for the week ahead. I use the cereal for snacks, for breakfast, and for the occasional treat when I'm in the mood. Later, when Mom goes into her room to rest her eyes, I double check to make sure her door is all the way closed. Then I get out my roll of shipping tape and one of my pre-written *if you find this balloon* notes and tape the note oh so carefully and securely onto the balloon. I keep the notes in my top dresser drawer. This is what they say:

If you are reading this, please write me a postcard saying so, and tell
me where you live.
I'm conducting a study of the wind.
Thank you very much.
Clarence J. Clark
600 N. Bishop Avenue, Apartment C,
Rolla, MO 65401

Next, I slip outside and set the balloon free. I let go of the ribbon and let the balloon fly up, up, until it's out of sight. I love this moment the most—stellar. I love just watching as the week's balloon is taken away on its own private journey to destination unknown. So far, I've launched twenty-three balloons and gotten back eight post cards, plus one actual letter. That's better than a 30% response rate, which is good if you take the time to calculate the odds against it staying filled with helium, or if you think of the likelihood of it getting caught in a tree or on an electric line, or of it popping who-knows-why in midair. Then there's the high chance that it will land and go unnoticed in the woods or by the side of a highway or in a vast body of water—just like the Chinese space station named Heavenly Palace that fell from the sky and splashed down in the Pacific Ocean on April 1, 2018. So, I feel like the 30% response is excellent.

Up to this point, the furthest a balloon has traveled has been St. Louis, nearly one hundred miles away. The Saturday I set that one free—it was green, the color Sheeree was giving out because of St. Patrick's Day—the temperature was around 50 degrees with a steady wind. The green, sham-rocked balloon floated up and up and up until it got pulled east. I could follow it with my eyes for a long, long time after I let go. Few sights are as indelible as that.

Under my bed I have a map, a Rand McNally of the United States, the school nurse gave me. She and I are tight. I see her every day when I go before lunch to take my medicine. Well, early last October she said she was going to throw out the map, said she was cleaning shop, and that I could have it if I wanted. I said, *most absolutely, yes sirree bob, that's just what I've been in the market for*. She gave me a wink, then rolled the map up neatly and put a brown rubber band around it. That night I mounted my new map onto one of those boards kids use for science fair projects. After I smoothed it and glued it all straight and everything, I got my box of pins. I bought all these necessary supplies with the money I made feeding Mom's boss's fish for an entire month while she was away *helping her dad die* is what she said.

So now, whenever I get a response from a balloon voyage, I mark the place where the postcard came from. The pins are technically called map pins, tiny with either red, yellow, green, or blue plastic beads for heads. This is important because two of the responses came from next-door neighbors behind the Walmart right here in Rolla. If the pins were any bigger, there's no way they'd fit.

The balloon that made it all the way to St. Louis landed in the front yard of a guy named Peter. He's the one who wrote me a letter. He must have had a fancy pen, probably a fountain pen, because the words had all these curlicues. The letter, which was on thick paper that said 100% cotton, looked almost like a painting. He said he was — enthralled is the word he used — by the wind, and that he keeps track of wind direction and velocity in his journal every single day. Then — get this — he asked what I did for a living. He wrote, *Are you a meteorologist or a graduate student at Missouri University of Science and Technology?* Finally, he said some stuff about himself. He's sixty-eight years old and has a dog, a black Labrador, who's named Linus after Snoopy's friend because his dog is all the time carrying around objects, sometimes even blankets, in his mouth. Peter mentioned that he's sad to be allergic to cats because he likes their independent nature. And then, maybe the strangest thing — besides the fact that someone I don't know wrote me a two-page letter — is how he ended it with a question: *Is anybody really listening anyway?* After the question, he had a little star — like this * — and another * at the bottom of the page with *The Who* written next to it. If someone asks you two questions, when they end their letter with a question, then they are most definitely looking for an answer. So, I plan to write Peter back and tell him I am ready to listen. If he is in the market for a listener, then I am the man for the job.

I have one clear obstacle to this entire project. Mom is almost always the one to get the mail, and she rips open envelopes without even checking to see whether they are addressed to her. This is one of her more annoying habits, and it would not be a good thing if she read Peter's response having no background info about this whole correspondence. First off, she will definitely have some big-time questions about why I've gotten a letter from a stranger in St. Louis. I need to break all this to her gradually, begin by explaining the balloon-setting-free experiment, how it feels to watch the balloon float up and up. She'll definitely get that. Next, I'll tell her about the map and the postcards. I'll tell her that the school nurse gave me the map, and that I made use of it by keeping an inventory of where my balloons have gone. I will also throw in the fact that I'm looking for some super-duper lightweight paper to write my next batch of notes on so they won't weigh down the balloons much at all. After that, I'll say that Peter was the only one to write me a real letter back. I think she'll be okay with it all if I explain it this way. And maybe she won't mind my having a pen pal. She's always wanting me to invite a friend over, or find a friend to hang out with, so she should be happy that I finally found one, even if he's in St. Louis.

Yesterday was warmer than usual, and after her nap Mom said we could do something fun together. So, we walked to Rolla Elementary to shoot hoops. We brought both basketballs, the Wilson I got for Christmas and the Spalding that had been in the lost and found for over a month at the YMCA where Mom works. She said she figured it was okay to scoop it out and bring it home for me. On the court, she'd pass a ball to me, then go after the one I'd just shot and throw it back to me. We got a good rhythm going. We did this over and over, probably over fifty times, until both of us were breathing hard and needing a break. So, we sat on the hillside next to the court and shared watered-down lemonade that she brought in my green Gatorade bottle. I'd take a sip, hand it to her. She'd take a sip, hand it back to me.

After that, we made up a game on the oversized map of the United States that's painted on the blacktop. It's there, I guess, so kids can keep up with the program even while they are at recess. Maybe the teachers think the states and their location will magically sink in while kids are tick tocking above the map on the swing set. The game we made up was that I'd jump and land on a state, Mom would throw me the ball, and I would have to say one fact I knew about the state. Then we'd switch. Most of my facts had to do with sports teams—The New York Dodgers, The California Raiders, The Illinois Blackhawks—but Mom knew some cool stuff. She said that in Vermont people have jobs as tree farmers. They grow acres and acres of maple trees and come late winter, when the temperature goes above freezing during the day but drops below at night, they gather the maple tree sap in metal buckets, then boil the sweet sap in huge trays until the water evaporates. It's all done in a building called a sugar shack, equipped with a hole in the roof so the steam can escape. What's left after the hours and hours of boiling is thick and sweet and mahogany in color, and that is maple syrup.

In Virginia, where Mom grew up, there's a sport called fox hunting. People get all dressed up—jackets and crisp white shirts, and a scarf-like thing called a stock tie—and ride horses who follow a pack of hounds which chase after the scent of a fox. If they come upon one, they scare the fox back to its den. Now that seems like a lot of fuss to me, but Mom said it is elegant to behold. She said she'd show me pictures of when she used to do it herself as a teenager. She said it was one of her happiest memories of being young. And she promised we'd go to both places, Virginia and Vermont—the "V" states—before I turn sixteen.

Mom works at the front desk of the YMCA on Thursdays and Saturdays from noon to eight. She also has a job as a will reader at Allen and Allen Law Offices. I've gone with her twice and waited as she sits in a windowless room that has an enormous and overly shiny wooden table. She and this lady, Mrs. Collins—who has wild, red hair in curls all over the place which makes it look like she has a perpetual, oversized halo—take turns reading out loud the wills of people who are not yet dead. If they find any mistakes in spelling, grammar, or punctuation, they circle those errors with a pen, just like a teacher would. Mom says the will-reading money we are saving for the "V" states adventure.

She's all the time saying that it's important to travel because what you end up finding out is more about yourself. She said you discover stuff you would never know if you just stayed home. And this information, she firmly believes, is what makes you *the best version of yourself.* That's how she says it, as if there were many versions we could choose. I'll have to keep on thinking on that one.

The only trip—like a get-on-a-plane trip—we've ever taken was to Maine to see the ocean and eat lobsters, as many as we could, anyway. We had gone to visit my uncle David, Mom's brother, but the first night I kept getting woken up by loud talking, talking as loud as yelling. And the next day we were on our own, heading to a different town. I was eight and what I remember most, besides the bibs we wore while eating lobsters, was flying. I got a hollow feeling in my stomach when the plane revved its engines on the runway and then after racing down the runway—clunk, wheels up—we were in the air, everything on the ground suddenly miniature, houses and buildings instantly becoming Monopoly pieces. It was amazing. The other brilliant thing was the flight attendant. Instead of the regular spiel you'd expect before a plane takes off, she made a hilarious skit. Here are some lines I remember pretty much word for word:

In a moment, the stewardess will be walking through the cabin to make sure your shoes and socks and purses all match;

As you know, this is a no smoking, no whining, no complaining flight. It's a please and thank you and you're good looking flight;

Now you can sit back and relax, or you can sit up and be tense — either way;

Next time you consider careening through the air in a steel canister, choose Southwest.

Everyone on the plane was doubled over, literally howling with laughter. It's like we all became friends because of what the flight attendant had said. Then here's what happened next. About twenty minutes into the flight, after the pilot announced we were at cruising altitude—I love the way he said it so official and all—the flight attendant came right to my seat, looked me in the eyes and said, *You are just the man I need.* The people sitting near us even turned their heads to check out what person she had chosen. Then she asked me if I wanted to help her pass out bags of pretzels. She explained that I would walk down the aisle and hand them to passengers while she poured their drinks. I guess she asked me because I was the only kid on that flight, except for one screeching baby. Still, it felt exceptional to get picked like that. I loved peering down at all the people in their seats, watching as they mulled over whether they wanted coffee or Coke or sparkling water.

MORE THAN I WISH TO ADMIT—SARAH

It's an old story. I'm lying to Clarence. I lie to him every day. He thinks my job is one thing, when really, it's another. I lie to him when I hide the fact that Henry left when I told him I was pregnant. We all know that children blame themselves. That's why I refuse to tell Clarence what he does not yet need to know. Clarence is better off the way he is. Would knowing his father didn't want a child serve any purpose? What Henry wanted none of was responsibility. But Clarence would naturally assume that his father left because he was different, because of his Asperger's.

My brother and his wife Whitney say I am abusing — that is the word they use — Clarence by withholding the truth. So, I have not spoken with them since I took Clarence to visit them in Maine. We stayed at their house only one night because Whitney, with her impeccably manicured nails and bright green eyes, made it perfectly clear that she and David would take it upon themselves to tell Clarence since I didn't have the backbone to do so. Early the next morning, I packed our bags, and we headed up the coast for the rest of our stay. The note I left said that I would tell Clarence in my own good time and they best stay out of my business. You can be sure that made Whitney's hair stand on end. Still, I'm sad to have cut off my brother like that. As children on rainy days, we'd sit in the back of his closet — the long walk-in kind — for hours. We'd sort buttons he kept in a mason jar, making a game of arranging them according to size. We'd sort out our lives, parse out what was going on, offer each other particles of hope. It's taken me decades to fit the pieces together enough to make sense of my mother's hard exterior. She kept everything from us. She wanted us to carry her resentment for her, to be suspicious of the world the way she was. I felt like a castaway on a boat that was oh-so-gradually sinking. My time with David in the closet was our lifeboat.

NO QUESTIONS ASKED—CLARENCE

I love the fact that if you become the pope, you get to choose your own name. You get a brand new one. You score an original name from what your parents gave you, a name all of your own making. The current pope chose the name Francis, which I like for a lot of reasons. Number one: we all know that Francis was the patron saint of animals. But did you know that he also came up with the idea for the first ever nativity scene? It was a living one. Just picture it: the 13th century and there stands Francis arranging people he thinks look like Mary and Joseph in a stable. How in the world did he get sheep, cattle, donkeys, and oxen to stay still, confined like that in such a compact space? You can be sure it was loud, quite the scene of mayhem, a lot of commotion and racket. But Francis did it. He made a real-life re-enactment of the night Jesus was born.

Another reason Francis is a great name is the book *Bread and Jam for Frances*. It features this badger who refuses to eat anything except bread and jam. Hoping to lure Frances into eating a wider variety of foods, her father, who is, of course, also a badger, oohs and ahhs about how great the soft-boiled egg he eats for breakfast is. But Frances sticks to her guns, no diet change. At school, she takes exquisite care with her cloth napkin on the lunch table, making the stark Formica look fit for a queen. Then she whips out the very same bread and jam getup she ate the day before. If you think about it, this really is a victorious story: a kid knows what she wants, what she likes, and won't be swayed by anyone into changing her mind. The third reason I like the name is Mom told me if I'd been a girl, she was going to call me Frances. The name has separate spellings: e for girls and i for boys. I think she was secretly glad I came out a boy. I could tell it by her voice when she said so.

I used to think the reason Mom got a frozen look on her face—like she'd eaten something ghastly—whenever I asked about my father was because he'd died a violent death she couldn't bear to talk about. This must have happened when I was young, before the age of one. Otherwise I'd remember at least some fact about him. I'd remember his smell, or the way he tied his shoes, or how he hummed while changing a light bulb. The first time I asked Mom, her entire body sort of seized up and shook, and I thought: you will remember this for a good long time. And sure enough, here I am over eight years with that moment still crystal clear in my mind. Because of her drastic reactions, mostly I've given up asking. It is flat-out no fun to see your mom look like something just bit her. It doesn't take much to figure that one out. So, I've come to terms with the fact that I will have to find out on my own who my father might be or might have been. Somehow this foldable man is a new clue I have to work with.

Not knowing a thing about my dad can get tricky. When people casually ask what my dad does—which seems a strange question— what someone does. I mean, what if a person literally just chewed gum all day, would you say *Well, he's a gum chewer*? Since I have no answer, part of me wants to make up an elaborate, untrue story. And one time I did. I said he was a traveling salesman; said he sold vinyl siding. I explained that he went door to door with a sample box hoping people would see the need to add a layer of protection onto the outside of their houses. I even explained that he offered five choices of siding colors: dove grey, white, Charleston green, barn red, and blue.

I'd researched all of this the week before when considering jobs that might take a dad away from home for long amounts of time. But when our principal—who'd asked—then asked where my father traveled, and I had no answer, that felt worse because he knew I was lying. For months afterwards I went to impressive lengths to avoid Dr. Roswell at all costs. If I saw him at the end of a hallway greeting kids on their way to lunch, I'd pretend I left something in the classroom and turn right around: woop.

So, when people ask about my dad, I try to change the subject. I make like I have suddenly spotted a rare and dazzling butterfly or heard a high-pitched sound we must all immediately investigate. If I draw attention to something in the nearby vicinity, usually my technique works. But I will say that my lack of an answer to the question occasionally gets some troubling reactions, some odd looks.

The one person I have told is Evan. He's in my language arts class. We sit next to each other. We were reading *Where the Red Fern Grows*, and Mr. Miller had told us to talk in groups about the part where Billy, who really, really wants those dogs, will come unhinged if he doesn't get them. So, there we were discussing what it feels like to want something you can't have, and Evan told our group in a roundabout way that he doesn't get to see his mom as much as he wants because she is in jail. He said his mom doesn't live with him and that he goes to see her every Sunday, and they spend 15 minutes together in a concrete room. I thought he was pretty brave to just blurt out something like that. I mean, talk about a gutsy thing to put out in the open for all to know.

So, after class I told him I didn't even know who my dad is or was. I said, *I'm collecting clues, but for the time being I have no genuine leads on who the dude is or even if he is.* I wanted to make it sound kind of light, the way he did about his mom; kind of casual, like it didn't matter that much in the greater scheme of things. Well, Evan stopped right there in his tracks and looked at me in a way that established we were friends, like a no-questions-asked kind of bond — no need to ever talk about it much more. It felt odd, this connection. But it also felt good. Evan did later mention that his mother's jail, Rolla Regional Jail, wasn't too bad except for the fact that the breakfast milk comes in plastic bags. He said there is no straw, just a bag of milk so it's nearly impossible to drink it. He didn't explain why his mom was in jail or what she had done. And I didn't ask.

TIME COLLIDES—SARAH

Airline wisdom: the closest exit may be behind you. Flight attendants say it so matter-of-factly, but if you think about it hard, this advice is useful in actual life too. Maybe your closest exit is actually in your past. Maybe the only way you can get out is by going backwards in time. What if, when I took the job as night custodian, I had just straight out told Clarence the truth about it? I kept it from him because I thought it would be hard for him to have to tell kids at school that his mom scrubbed toilets for a living, but now that I've gotten this far into my story, securing the mannequin so it looks like someone's reading in the front room every night, I realize what I've done might be far, far worse. I think Clarence would see that I had taken this job so I can be there for him most afternoons when he gets home. Plus, he's old enough to understand the need to make money where and how you can.

Time collides is what I thought to myself last night. People say time flies, but that's far too gentle, way too breezy. People say time passes, but that is too peaceful. Rarely is time spread out all nice and neat like a quilt for a picnic on a summer lawn. Of the tasks I do at First Baptist, vacuuming is my favorite. First off, I like it that the machine is called a shark and that it's red: power and danger all wrapped in one. And I derive satisfaction from how it sucks up things you couldn't see were even there. The rug in the sanctuary is also red, so the corner of Sunday's bulletin or a crumb of a communion wafer—those you see. But there are the darker objects—the back to an earring, the tip of a pencil, even one time a necklace—that remain invisible until the shark sucks them up. If I hear a loud noise, I stop and open up the reservoir and see if I can retrieve the vacuumed object. That's how I found the ruby necklace.

I enjoy vacuuming because the hum of the machine cancels out what's swirling in my head. That's what I mean by time colliding. But for those minutes of vacuuming, I don't think. I don't worry. Time doesn't collide, doesn't smash into itself quite as audibly, when there is the hum of a vacuum. After I get back from cleaning the church, washing windows and putting away dishes in the fellowship hall kitchen, it's hard to fall back to sleep before I need to get Clarence up for school. So, this is when I do a kind of thinking that is more than thinking, a thinking smooth as velvet.

I've had the church job for over a year, and I've got the timing down pretty much to a T. I leave the apartment right around midnight once I'm certain Clarence will not wake until morning. Ever since he was out of diapers, he'd need to go to the bathroom a couple hours after bed. And he still stumbles half asleep down the narrow corridor to the bathroom we share. Occasionally though, he comes into my room insisting that the dream he's had—almost always about being chased by hulking birds, birds much larger than any he's seen in actual life—is true. On those nights, it's like I have to erase the fears. I tell him to start with his toes and move up through his body—feet, ankles, shins, thighs, belly, back, shoulders, neck—and to instruct that part of him to sleep, sleep, sleep. If he imagines the words in his mind, he may lull himself to sleep before he even gets above his knees. I tell him the more specific the part, the better. He can even command each toe, one at a time: baby toe, next to baby toe, middle toe.

While I sit on the side of his bed whispering *sleep sweetly sweet Clarence* under my breath, he is a young boy again, six or seven, and I wish hard for this moment to never end. There is nothing more I want in the world than this exact moment. The sleep comes to him gradually, the way a barge moves, but eventually his breathing deepens, widens, filling the cells of his body. I know he will stay asleep until morning. This is when it is okay for me to set up the mannequin; to leave and go on in to work.

UNANSWERABLE QUESTIONS—CLARENCE

There are many. As far as I can tell, no one knows what happens after we die or if there is life on other planets. I cannot figure out why Mom has Fred, the foldable man, or who my father is — or was. Then there are the smaller mysteries. Yesterday when I was practicing my fishing casting at Bear State Park (I used two washers on my rod and just cast into the short grass) a little girl on the back of her dad's bike passed me on the path, and I overheard only a parcel of her song: *Up above the world so high like a diamond in the sky*. We all know those words come from the song Twinkle, Twinkle Little Star, but did she sing the entire thing through, start to finish? Was she singing it over and over and over like I used to?

If I were given three wishes, my first would be to have an unlimited number of wishes. That's one way to beat the system. It's funny how we say wishes come true, but we don't say hopes come true. Guess that's how different wishing and hoping are. I better be careful never to flip-flop them in my mind. Hoping seems less urgent, of less import, like *I hope it doesn't rain during the baseball game, or I hope she didn't forget her lunch*. We don't really wish those things. Wishes are like prayers, like you are directly asking for help from someone bigger than yourself.

We're studying World War I in history class. Those guys in the trenches really had a terrible time of it. There was, however, one bright spot. It was the Christmas Truce of 1915, which all began when one brave German soldier walked over to the British lines carrying a white flag. In case you don't know, a white flag means truce; it means *let's stop fighting*. When the British understood what that soldier was offering, they all let go of the tight feelings, set down their guns and hoisted themselves out of the trenches. Then these enemies played soccer together under light cast by flares. They showed each other pictures of their wives and mothers. They shared chocolate and cigarettes, sang songs and played musical instruments. They had a party together for that one night, but the next day went back to fighting.

Let's wander in and see what else we can see is what the substitute language arts teacher — Mr. Selby — said today before it was time to do popcorn reading. He made it sound like books are rooms there for us to discover: see what we can see, wander in. Before that, he helped us correctly say his name; he said he wasn't a carton of milk with a sell by date and we shouldn't pronounce it that way: it's sell bee, not sell by. I always think it kind of puts everyone at ease when there's a splendid joke. With Mom, when she's staring out the window, a joke can switch things up pretty quickly. So, I try to keep a storehouse of jokes I can crack for her when necessary. Here's one: What did Adam say on the day before Christmas? It's Christmas, Eve. Today's literary term was oxymoron, which means a contradiction in terms. The example Mr. Selby gave was giant shrimp. That's a tough one to forget. He also said happy family was an oxymoron, and then he kind of winced. I must think that one over.

THE WORLD I'D LIKE TO INVENT—SARAH

Clarence is in his room sorting pieces of paper and weighing them in his hands. *Is notebook paper lighter than newspaper? No. Is construction paper heavier than the paper of a grocery bag? Yes.* I hear him in there talking to himself. It's very sweet and interior. Then, he comes out and asks me what I think is the lightest paper in the world. *Tissue paper*, I say, *or maybe lens cleaning paper*. But he just shakes his head and says, *Well, those won't work*. And I know better than to ask, *Work for what*? If he's got a project under his sleeve, it is best for me to stay clear out of his way. So, I go into my room and open the trunk I keep in the back corner of my closet, where I just happen to still have some honest to goodness typing paper I'd saved from my college days. I saved it for its smell and the fact that each sheet has a watermark. When I hand him the box of typing paper, he opens it slowly like it's a treasure and he wants to savor this moment of finding out what the treasure might be. And I can tell by the look on his face that this is exactly what he had in mind. He spins around, goes back to his room, and closes the door triumphantly.

In the world I'd invent, we'd talk about books the way we do about people. We'd gossip about all their details; we would pick them apart — their bad hairdos and mismatched socks — instilling the books with great significance. We'd bring them up in casual conversation while in line at the bank. They'd walk around with us, these books, becoming part of our most essential selves. Second thing in my invented world: a lot more silence. The world is far too noisy, filled with useless sound. We've gotten so uncomfortable with silence we even use the word awkward before it: awkward silence. Now, how does that work? Maybe what came before the moment of silence was awkward — even doomed — but the silence itself is not. How can it possibly be? Silence is a beautiful thing unto itself, spacious, with room to rest.

When I was waiting for Clarence to be born, well into my eighth month, early one morning I set out on my day off from work, to just walk. I walked out of Rolla's city limits, walked to where the roads narrow and the houses become sparser but somehow feel more loved, the single geranium plant and close-cut lawn so tenderly cared for. My mother called this phenomenon 'house proud', people taking pride in what they own. But it somehow seems more than that, more than pride. It's as if their house is definitely a home and there's no other place in the world they'd rather be for the time they're granted on this earth. So, they will tend this one thing as lovingly as they can.

By early afternoon of that day, I was so thirsty I garnered my courage and knocked on the door of a trailer tucked into some tall pines beside the road, hoping for a glass of water. The woman who answered wore a yellow-flowered apron and the glass she handed me had red cherries on it. As I drank the water in the doorway, she picked up a pear from her table. She walked over to me, stood very close and then pressed the flawless yellow fruit up to my belly. All of this she performed in silence. She closed her eyes for what felt like many minutes. When she opened them, she said my baby would have a birthmark in the shape of a pear. She said it would be something perpetually lovely on the child. And that's all she said. She didn't speak when I asked for water, didn't ask my name or anything. She just held the pear to my belly and made that proclamation, that prediction. And sure enough, right behind Clarence's left earlobe is a pear-shaped mark, tiny and glorious. It is one of the many unique and magnificent things about him.

EVERYTHING ENDS SOMETIME—CLARENCE

Mom sent me to Kroger to pick up one lemon, three avocados and some garlic. She said she would make guacamole to go with our tacos. So, there I was in the produce section, picturing in my mind how avocado's leathery skin is a lot like a baseball glove. But I couldn't get to the avocados because there was this guy standing dead center in front of the bin, filling bag after bag with avocados. I was 99% sure he was out to buy them all. So, I cleared my throat the way adults do when they want to get a point across. But the avocado dude just kept on bagging, acting like he didn't even hear me. This is when I lifted my lanyard which has three keys — apartment key, mailbox key, and bike lock key — to make a startling, clinking sound. But that still did not do the trick. I peered into his cart to discover he was buying what seemed like all the produce he could: red peppers, lettuce, carrots, squash, celery; you name it. What in the world was he going to do with all those vegetables? Finally, I wedged myself between him and the remaining avocados and grab three. I felt lucky to get even those.

Everything ends sometime. That's what Mom says when things get hard. If I tell her how I don't like the substitute in PE because all he lets us do is dribble the ball and stand in line to wait to shoot, she says, *Everything ends sometime, Clarence.* When you think of it, that fact can be good or bad news, depending on the circumstance. I never want bowling to end, for instance, or the way it feels when you wake up and are kind of floating, your arms smooth and weightless, as the sunlight comes into the room and you don't have to go to school that day. I want that feeling to last forever, to never end.

Wayne's Lanes is the only bowling alley in Rolla, and I love the smell of it. It's a mixture of summer and bacon, all wrapped together with a bit of cotton candy. The brilliant thing about bowling is that you are part of the lane next to you the whole time. So, if the next lane over is having a party, you are at the party, too. One time the birthday boy even brought us slices of his ice cream cake. He was having a total blast, spinning in circles each time he watched his ball meander down the lane. It was like a movie scene in slow motion. Even if he missed, he'd spin on the leather-soled shoes, spin in this crazy way like there was nowhere in the world he'd rather be. Truth be told, that was the best part of bowling that day: watching that kid being so happy to be who and where he was.

I got up the courage to tell Mom about the balloons, and the notes, and the map, and Peter. It felt good to just spill it all out. And she didn't seem at all fazed about the balloons. She said I was enterprising — her word — to come up with such an idea. But she was not too keen about my writing to a stranger we didn't know the first thing about. And when she heard that he was an English professor, she seemed to stiffen a little. No, she stiffened a lot. She definitely stiffened a lot and sucked in her breath like she'd just come up from being under water and urgently needed oxygen. So, I decided to just up and show her the letter Peter had sent me. For a long time, she sat at the kitchen table reading it, looking at the handwriting, staring into space. She slowly copied down his address on the comic section of the day's paper, between *Peanuts* and *Calvin and Hobbes*. Then she went back to her room. At least that's over, I thought to myself. Everything ends sometime.

PITCH CLEAR AND TO THE POINT—SARAH

Clarence told me of a project he has undertaken. He is setting helium balloons free and keeping track of where they land on a map. He ties a note onto each balloon and asks the finder to write him a note back. His ingenuity seems boundless. But a feeling came upon me unawares, a feeling of great trepidation, my heart rate rising, when he told me he had gotten a letter back from a professor in St. Louis. For a brief flash of time, I felt sure it was Henry who'd found the balloon and written Clarence back. I felt sure that something more than serendipity had intervened. But I was wrong—thankfully. It was not Henry. It was a community college professor named Peter who seems sweet and old-fashioned. So, I think Clarence's experiment might just bring about something good for him.

After I followed Henry to Rolla, I got a job teaching American literature to 11th graders at Barnstable High School while he taught writing at Missouri University of Science and Technology. I had some remarkable students. I still remember this one essay Caitlin Call wrote on *Moby Dick*. While the vast majority of essays were about hidden meanings in the book, overly wrought analyses of Melville, this paper began with the simple declarative sentence: *Moby Dick is a really long book about an extremely big fish.* Talk about being pitch clear and to the point. And the rest of Caitlin's essay followed suit. It was so funny and light it gave new meaning to this classic book. That's one thing I miss most about teaching, how students will see the world in a new way. This widens your world. I also loved getting to see the lights go on in students when we talked about themes in books. Whether or not you believe it, everyone has their eyes open. It's just whether we choose to see what's right in front of us that makes the difference.

I only got to teach for five months here in Rolla because the high school's principal did not appreciate the way I ran a classroom. In fact, he had never heard of John Dewey and Progressive education. So, the January day I had the students build tents out of quilts I'd brought in and write in their journals by flashlight, the principal called me into his office and reprimanded me for being too casual in my pedagogy. He said I needed to be more formal in my classroom management. And that was something I am afraid I could not do. I do dearly miss the students and the savoring of delightful books. One of my favorite assignments — one I would begin each year with — was Eudora Welty's luminous review of *Charlotte's Web*. Here is what Miss Welty wrote in October 1942.

Charlotte's Web has liveliness and felicity, tenderness and unexpectedness, grace and humor and praise of life, and the good succinctness that only the most highly imaginative stories seem to grow.

Wilbur is of sweet nature. He is a spring pig, affectionate, responsive to the moods of the weather and the song of the crickets, has long eyelashes, is hopeful, partially willing to try anything, brave, subject to faints from bashfulness, is loyal to friends, enjoys a good appetite and a soft bed, and is a little likely to be overwhelmed by the sudden chance for complete freedom.

Charlotte A Cavitica ("but just call me Charlotte") is the heroine, a large gray spider. She has eight legs and can wave them in friendly greeting. When her friends wake up in the morning she says, "Salutations"-in spite of sometimes having been up all night herself, working.

What the book is about is friendship on earth, affection and protection, adventure and miracle, life and death and the passing of time. As a piece of work it is just about perfect and just about magical in the way it is done. "At-at-at the risk of repeating myself," as the goose says, "Charlotte's Web is an adorable book."

Another writer, Kevin Kling, said, *As children we are closer to our creator.* I think that is dead-on accurate, one of those simultaneously astonishing yet obvious facts. We are closer in time to whatever force made us. We were just there, near the sacred. All children recently rubbed shoulders with whatever or whoever gave us spirits and intuition, compassion and the ability to love. And this brings to mind another one of my favorite quotations. It's by Louis Pasteur, the brilliant inventor of <u>pasteurization</u>: *When I approach a child, he inspires in me two sentiments: tenderness for what he is, and respect for what he may become.* I say that quotation, those words, over and over in my head. I repeat them and still feel something new each time.

Clarence is still far too tender to hear that his father ran off with a student half his age the moment I told him I was pregnant. How can that be shared in the right way? To Clarence, that truth would be clamorous and haunting. And so, though I withhold that truth, some might say I am being untruthful, I'll wait until he is older, not as close to his creator. At least that's what I tell myself, and it works for now. I mean who would want to grow up thinking someone close to you didn't want you? It takes a lot to offset that.

Sometimes I mix up my actual life with the lives I read about in books. If I enter the lives of a novel's characters, then my own troubles dim in comparison. Call my reading an addiction, but at least it's one I can live with. Henry would listen to my retelling of books without judgement, without questions, without comment. It was the kind of listening that made you recognize that you were truly being heard. That is what I miss most about him: the way he would listen and not try to take the pain away, just share in it with me, just let me be. And who among us does not wish for that?

Across the street I watch the lady who lives in Bear Park push a Kroger grocery cart filled with cans of cat food. She's on her way to feed the strays she calls her own. When I asked her, one afternoon in February — I had stopped the car when I saw her huddled against an oak tree — if I could take her to the Salvation Army Shelter for the night as it was forecast to be in the low teens, she shook her head fiercely. She said her cats would be lost without her. They wouldn't know what to do if she wasn't there with their food come morning. I'm glad for her assuredness that she is so definitely needed in this life. She's lucky to have that.

Henry never wanted to marry, so I should have seen what was coming. I should have known that a child would not seal the deal but would turn our relationship in the opposite direction from what I had in mind. But at thirty-six you sense your biological clock ticking mighty fast. And ever since I can remember, I had wanted a child, someone to love unconditionally. Even as a young girl I remember an ache in my bones, a kind of yearning to hold a baby in my arms. I'd go over to our neighbor's just so I could help with their toddler, lift the tiny rubber-tipped spoon to his mouth and watch as he half ate pureed sweet potatoes and apricots, food miraculously bright. When Henry started acting differently, I didn't want to admit it to myself, so I ignored all the classic signs: a new aftershave that smelled like musk, additional office hours, faculty meetings that popped up out of nowhere.

WRONG BOX ON THE ANSWER SHEET—CLARENCE

One thing about adults is how they are always asking what I want to be when I grow up. Part of me wants to say, *myself*—I want to be myself when I grow up. After the person asking me poses that question—and often before I've had a chance to answer—he or she will go on and on about how much they miss being a kid. Their eyes get dreamy, and you can tell they've gone back in time and are remembering a specific moment from when they were eleven or twelve. It's like their childhoods were perfect, Leave It to Beaver or Father Knows Best families and communities. When Mom and I watch reruns of those shows, it strikes me as highly unlikely that dinner was always at six and that there was a front hall with a hat rack where everyone hung their coats and scarves neatly first thing after they walked in the door. What are the odds of that happening?

My stock answer, when asked, is that I want to be a shoe shiner, or what the internet calls a bootblack. The way I see it, you can get a job doing that pretty much anywhere in the world. You'd meet people who are going places, people who need something basic. No complex surgery that might go wrong, no fire to put out, no gymnasium full of screaming kids playing dodge ball. And for however long you take to shine the person's shoes, he or she would talk with you, maybe even about their personal life. Whenever I say this, though—about the shoeshine job—the adult who asks quickly changes the topic, gives me a look as if I checked the wrong box on the answer sheet.

Another cool job would be that of a stage prompter. You'd stand out of sight behind the heavy green velvet curtain, and when an actor forgot a line, you'd get to supply the missing words. You'd be a full-time superhero, constantly rescuing people who are stuck. There's the actor about to panic and you put that fire right out.

Well, get this, the drama teacher at school came up to me two weeks ago in the cafeteria and asked if I would like to be a prompter for the spring production of *The Wizard of Oz*. He said if an actor forgets a line — which is a fact I'll know because they'll stop talking and the whole play will come to a complete standstill — I'll just feed them a couple lines with my loud whisper voice. Your job will be to kind of wind up the play, is what he said, the way you wind up a toy and if it winds down, you wind it up again. For the stage prompting, I'll have to stay after school until 5:30 and give characters their lines during rehearsal. I like the plot of *The Wizard of Oz*. I like how Dorothy has all these adventures, but they are actually just taking place in her own mind. My favorite character is the scarecrow who seems believable. I understand the way he is even scared of being scared, how he is freaked out by the littlest things, and yet just keeps on plodding along telling himself to keep going.

Last year our class performed *Doctor Dolittle*. The first outstanding thing — besides the title itself — is how the play takes place in Puddleby-on-the-Marsh. Talk about an original name. Plus, Doctor Dolittle's friends are animals: Gub-Gub, the pig; Dab Dab the Duck; Too-Too, the owl. And then there is the great combination animal, Pushmi-Pullu, who is a gazelle-unicorn mix with two heads. How great would that be to have such an assorted and original group of friends to call your own? The play began as a series of letters that this guy, Hugh Lofting, wrote to children, complete with illustrations and all. He did this when he was a soldier; he wrote the entire thing in the trenches in Spain during World War I. When an interviewer asked him how he came up with the idea, he said the actual news was too horrible and too dull. So, he made up this entire other world.

LEAVE YOUR PRAYERS ON THE TABLE—SARAH

Truth be told, I rarely feel lonely. I've got Clarence. We have each other. It's all working out much better than I ever thought. I've tried some dating sites over the years, started answering those interminable, persistent online forms. But somehow it just never clicked. I found the questions too straightforward, too canned. They did not allow for any wiggle room. Here are some examples: *Do I like drama or romance movies? The beach or the mountains? Am I a believer?* I would talk to myself out loud as I tried to fill in the forms: *hum, what is better, the beach or the mountains? Well, I like the waves and water, but the mountains transport you. Am I a believer? A believer in what? In the healing powers of chocolate: definitely yes. In God? I'm pretty sure, yes. In a God fenced in by an organized religion? Definitely no.* A few months ago Clarence walked in the room while I was talking to myself as I filled out one of those forms. I didn't hear him, so I don't know how long he stood still in there listening. But when I said, *Are you a smoker?* And Clarence answered, *That you are, Mom.* I felt both ashamed and sad. I need to quit this smoking. I need to do that soon.

I gave a lot of serious thought to moving last spring. I applied for jobs all over and was even a finalist for a job at a girls' boarding school in North Carolina. But I just couldn't do it. Clarence has gained traction here in Rolla. He has found a comfortable enough routine: school during the week, Kroger outings every Saturday, projects like his owl, basketball, and baseball. It's safe for him to bike around here so he even has a good bit of freedom. And this might sound strange, but he's found a father figure of sorts in Larry who manages the Rent-to-Own next door. When Clarence goes over there after school, Larry makes sure he's comfortable, gives him popcorn and a coke, and tells him to make himself at home. I don't want to take him away from what is working for him. So, for the time being, we will do what my mother called "making do". She'd say, *Sarah, sometimes you just have to make do. Sometimes that's the only option you have.* That was one of the rare true and useful things she ever said.

When my plane was delayed on my way back from my job interview in Charlotte, I wandered into the airport chapel before noon mass, and the priest gave me a laminated prayer page and told me to talk to Jesus. I am not kidding you. All I could think of was the menu at Waffle House and how it is kind of a prayer page. All those choices, so much possibility. I'm sure the priest did not want me thinking of it this way; but how can you keep yourself from a thought? I still haven't figured that one out and here I am forty-eight years old. And I still definitely can't get over that laminated prayer page. How many hands had touched it? How many people have been instructed by it, while traveling, to talk to Jesus? I stayed in the airport chapel right until the service started, then slipped out. I left the prayer page on the table with all the rest.

RETURN TO THE REAL WORLD—CLARENCE

My favorite puzzle is "connect the dots". At first, you're focused on following the number sequence, making the line from three to four, from four to five, from five to six as straight and clear as you possibly can. But then, gradually, there emerges a seal balancing a ball on its nose, or a mermaid, or a Christmas tree. In my experience, these pictures always contain a bit of marvel. They have a fantastical nature to them. They are not everyday objects: no toothbrushes or bathtubs or school buses. Plus, the way the image slowly appears holds an undeniable magic. Connect the dots allows you to slowly discover a hidden truth. It is an unfurling, a gradual clarification. As the truth emerges, there is a momentary sense of being wise. The moment burgeons, escalates, becomes almost otherworldly.

About four times a year, Mom and I go see a movie together. In my mind, there are four reasons to go to the movies. We all know you can rent a movie later—once it's had its stint on the big screen—and watch it from the comfort of your own home. Peaches likes to wedge herself on the couch beside me if I have a movie on the television. She falls asleep pretty much straight away, right when the actual movie starts. She sometimes even snores. It sounds like sawing and has a warmth to it. It's actually very comforting. So, it's hard to justify paying $8.50 to see what you can watch later in a more relaxed kind of way.

Reason one to go to the movies is the popcorn, which tastes better there than anyplace else in the world. Reason number two is the way everyone sits together in one room, all focused on the same thing. How often do you encounter that in real life? Maybe it happens when there is an accident on the highway, and the traffic comes to a standstill and everyone cranes their necks to see what has happened. They call this rubber necking. And occasionally it happens in school when a kid gets in trouble, and the teacher turns his or her attention on that one kid.

Unless the punishment is bad enough to send the kid out of the room, there is a moment when everyone is utterly silent and staring, listening to what the teacher is saying—and to the kid. Everyone stops and focuses on them. Let's just say that in our digital age, everyone focusing at the same time on the same thing is not an everyday occurrence.

Reason number three for movie going is watching the previews. When Mom and I see a movie, we make a game of rating the previews. After one preview ends, we tap out on each other's knee a score for what we would give that upcoming movie. Our rating scale runs from one to ten. One means there is no way we'll shell out the dough to see it, seven and up: we've got to see it. Nine and ten means we'll put it on the calendar to make certain we go see it. We almost always rate previews the same. We are never more than one point apart. The major difference is Mom doesn't like action scenes or dark tunnels, and I most definitely do.

The final movie-going reason I will call the thrill ride. It's the pre-show advertisement where you are on a roller coaster surrounded by gargantuan—word collection word—popcorn exploding loudly and unrealistically. Of course, they're trying to get you to go back out to the lobby and buy an overly priced drink and some candy, but I see it as a free mini thrill. Usually I get dizzy. One time I yelled.

Mom says it makes her sad when a movie ends, and she has to return to the real world. She wishes time in actual life would happen just the way it does in movies with the good parts lasting a long, long time and the bad ones over in the blink of an eye. After our last matinee show, she announced that she was absolutely and definitely never going to see a movie during the daytime again. She said it was the most depressing thing in the world to walk back out into the light of day and to face the wakened world after the haze of a movie. I can kind of see her point, even though for me the world often seems as technicolored as the movies.

NO ONE IS FOOLED—SARAH

Growing up, I never had to worry about money. I went to private schools, learned to ballroom dance at cotillion, fox hunted on the weekends, the whole nine yards. I try to keep this from people I meet here in Rolla as I figure it will only create a distance between us that will forever be hard to bridge. My friends at the "Y" might well think I am a phony. Plus, living with old wealth can come with some burdensome expectations. The best way to explain why that is so is to conjure up the image of a ventriloquist and his dummy—a word I detest. When there is a ventriloquist, the audience is meant to believe the puppet (dummy) is the one speaking the script. But underneath it all, no one is really fooled. Everyone knows who is doing the talking. The puppet is expected to say what the puppeteer can't or won't or hasn't the heart to. We all can see straight through that gloss and fanfare, to what is hiding behind it all. Well, in some wealthy families there may be even more of a show that is hiding something deeply corrosive. There's the mother who's an alcoholic, but everyone pretends it's not really a problem. There is the father who's more in love with his money than he is with his children. Put it this way: it's far easier to see through ventriloquism than it is the gloss of the ultra-privileged. They can be experts at hiding the truth.

The history of ventriloquism is enthralling. This art of changing one's voice to make it seem as if it is coming from someone else is ancient. The Greeks believed these sounds to be the voices of the dead. And they regarded the ventriloquist as divine, able to speak to the dead and tell the future. At the Temple of Delphi, the priestess Pythia would stand stock still, her mouth unmoving, and the audience believed that what emanated from her motionless mouth were the words of sacred oracles uttered by the god Apollo. When I explained all this to Clarence, I could tell it made an impression on him. Speaking of this, it recently occurred to me that the word emotion and the word motion both mean to be moved.

When my father died leaving all his money to his new wife — the one he'd abandoned us for — my mother rolled up her sleeves, dug into her determination, got a full-time job in an office and assured me we'd be just fine. And we were. You might think it was a huge fall from grace or comfort, but in some ways it was a genuine relief as we were instantly freed from so many of the expectations and trappings of the wealthy. I remember the day like it was yesterday. I was twelve and my mother was leaning against the kitchen sink shaking her head, mumbling, *I will not do such a thing,* over and over. When I ask, *What won't you do?* she answers, *I will not contest your father's will. I will not argue that he was of unsound mind when he wrote his will out on a legal pad by hand. We will make do just fine without his money.* Above her, the overhead fan churned the air, and she rocked from foot to foot, her fists clenched tightly like she was holding something no one could make her let go of. Remembering this, I see that she was holding fast to something. She was grasping her pride. She would not rely on anyone else. She would make do.

I want to get this story right, so let me try again. My mother would frequently — almost daily — quote Abraham Lincoln. She would say we should always strive to be in the presence of the better angels of our nature.[1] And she firmly believed that the trappings of the upper class were roadblocks to those angels. She'd grown up having to wear long white gloves and be a debutante when at heart she was fiercely independent and down to earth. She was proud of doing things herself, of not needing anyone or anything else. She was both self-contained and resigned.

As a result, our relationship had a certain formality. It was a relationship that wouldn't allow for intimacy, that kept us at a distance from each other. So, you might see why I couldn't bring myself to tell her when I became pregnant with Clarence. It's not that I was too young or irresponsible, it was simply that we didn't talk about things like that. At thirteen, when I had my first period, she handed me an enormous

---

[1] Lincoln's First Inaugural Address

bag of maxi pads along with a booklet explaining what happens during menstruation. Then she walked away as if it were a business transaction.

We never talked about things that might hurt. We kept the topics neutral: the weather or how the neighbors had mowed their grass far too short, and it worried her it might get scorched in July's sun. So, it wasn't until I started showing with Clarence and was planning to visit her for the weekend that I casually dropped the news, like it was a movie I planned to see, or like it was just a fact that barely mattered to me. And she responded in kind: *Well, when's it due?* And that was all we said of it. She didn't ask if I was seeing someone. She didn't ask who the father was or if I had a boyfriend. She just asked when the baby was due to be born.

Exquisitely, my mother could rattle off random and remarkable facts all day long: how if sheep eat too much clover their bellies will burst, how cows stand up and sit down an average of fourteen times a day. She knew that the Dewey Decimal system allowed libraries to shelve books according to topic rather than alphabetically, or by time of acquisition, or date of publication. She had at the tip of her tongue all the myriad meanings of the word "tender": caring, kindhearted, soft, coal car, boat used to ferry people and supplies to and from a ship, an offer of money. Almost everything she said had a kind of truth that you could rely upon, a kind of direction for life. And she had a saying for most every situation: *the darkest night brings the brightest dawn; a stitch in time saves nine; as you sow, so shall you reap.* Maybe these proverbs anchored her, helped her stay in the world by sticking to the wisdom of words rather than trudging into the shark-filled waters of the every day.

VANISHING POINT—CLARENCE

If you are looking down a straight road, it appears smaller and smaller to the eye until it is teeny tiny. It becomes nearly invisible. So, if you are drawing a road, you make the lines closer and closer together in the distance to show this happening. This is called the vanishing point. And this same vanishing experience happens to me when I watch my balloons float out of sight in the sky. Briefly I leave the world I can see, and I enter another one. I visit the world of the traveling balloon. Try it sometime and see if that happens to you. It's worth the sacrifice of the balloon, I assure you that.

Mom says there are no photographs of miracles, that those unexpected and wondrous events unexplainable by science or logic, are fleeting and not one has ever been captured in a photograph. I like that fact, that they are temporary and made even more wonderful because of that. It's a bit how I feel about my freed balloons.

I wrote back to Peter, having waited a week so I would not appear overly eager. Here is what I said:

Dear Peter,

Thank you for the letter. To tell you the truth, yours is only the fourth letter I've gotten in my entire life, and the other three were from my grandmother. I bet St. Louis is a cool place to live. My mom and I go there sometimes so she can stand for what seem like hours in front of a painting by Winslow Homer. It shows kids in a schoolroom and their teacher, all reading. After the art museum, we usually go to City Museum, which is like a gigantic, indoor playground. There's even a 10-story slide. I am in the seventh grade. My backpack is heavy, and my locker is in an entirely different hallway from all my classes, so I lug all my books around with me rather than risk being late to a class.

Your dog sounds exceptional. I would love to have a dog, but for now we're dog-less, Mom and me. We do have a cat though. Her name is Peaches, and she loves to stare out the window and watch the world go by.

Well, that's about it. I am excited to have a pen pal.

Sincerely,
Clarence Clark

Although Peter might be a good person to tell that Mom is keeping a folded man in a box under her bed, I figure I will wait until the next letter to ask if he knows anything about mannequins. While we're on the subject, and to make things easier, I will give Mom's man-in-a-box an actual name. It might make the entire thing a little less sketchy. I'll call him Fred, Fred the foldable man. But I'm still sure it's definitely better to wait to bring up the topic with Peter. You don't want to rush into things too quickly.

The reason I told Peter about the Winslow Homer painting is because it's famous, featuring kids — most of them barefoot — sitting on wooden benches. I think what Mom likes most about it is how kids of varying ages are all together in a room reading. I'm 99% sure it's her idea of heaven on earth. Children, books, quiet — her favorite things — together in one safe place. Mom used to be a teacher here at Rolla High, but one day the principal came in and found her and her students on the floor under some quilts she'd stretched over desks placed in a circle. Her students were all reading and writing in their journals. They were using lanterns and flashlights, even headlamps. The principal fired her that very day, told her it was not appropriate huddle in the dark like that. I secretly hate that principal for it. He did not understand what my mother was trying to do, that she was trying to get her students to feel cozy and at home. She was trying to get them to love reading the way she does.

I have a different taste in art than Mom. Me? I like flashy colors. There's this guy in Peru who paints underwater while underwater. I'm not kidding. He dives into the ocean with everything he needs, using oil paint to capture on canvas the brightly decorated fish who glide by. How great would that be to have a job cruising around the reefs and painting what you see? In an interview, he said painting underwater was his dream when he was a kid. He wrote, *All my life I wanted to do something different. I wanted to see for myself, with my own eyes, the depths of the sea.*[2] I bet you'd sort of feel like you yourself had vanished, the colors and sights around you so dazzling and intense as to draw you into oneness with all you are seeing.

I think whoever my dad is would like flashy colors too. I just sort of have that feeling about him. After I read on the internet about the underwater painter, I stayed in the research mode and tried to find out more about mannequins. Instead, I stumbled upon a site all about wax museums. These are buildings filled with human look-alikes made entirely out of wax. The figures appear calmer than humans who are sleeping, stilled like water in a river's eddy where it swirls gently amid some rapids. Some historical figures who've been made of wax include Abe Lincoln, Joe DiMaggio and Rosa Parks. Some contemporary ones are Justin Bieber, Michael Jordan, and Hillary Clinton. Doesn't that strike you as odd that someone has gone to the trouble to make Justin Bieber out of wax? Just take a moment to think that one through. Why make a wax figure of a wax figure? I hope they don't make one of Donald Trump. That would be alarming.

Speaking of wax and stillness, sometimes I just hang out in Stone Gate Cemetery. If you think about it, graveyards are wide open, welcoming spaces, like playgrounds, but without the worry of kids screaming and running into you. There are two graveyards in Rolla, not counting the ones behind churches. There's Holly Memorial Gardens on the hill next to Walmart, and then there's Stone Gate where a lot of the grave sites have solar powered lights set up on them. At night, it looks like a million fireflies — colorful ones — have called a group meeting. Last summer I rode my bike there to check out what the lights looked like during the day, and I can tell you some gravestones are really decked out. There are solar powered lights literally cemented to the stones. A few graves are just enormous crosses, all studded with lights.

---

[2] Patrick Mimbela

One grave is in the shape of a butterfly with purple, pink, and magenta lights. On the stone are written the words *Infant Daughter Morris*, but there are no dates or other identifying details. I didn't know what to make of it. Part of me found it sweet, like they think she is now a lit butterfly, but another part of me felt it would be strange to be a lit butterfly after you're dead.

Truth be told, there are people you know are alive — but are dead to you, like my dad. And there are people who go through the motions of living but don't give life to anyone else. And that is definitely not being light, not lit up, no way, not one bit. I enjoy reading the quotations some people choose for their stones. Mom says they are called epitaphs, and that they are most often verses from the Bible. But I've found three that are not: *Don't cry because it's over, smile because it happened; Gone but not forgotten*; and the best one — *Gone fishing*. Stone Gate graveyard is vast, the size of a few football fields at least. So, it will take me quite a few more visits to cover its entire span, and I'm hopeful I'll find more memorable quotes.

Behind Stone Gate is a lake. While I was busy inspecting graves, a pair of geese landed in the water, and another pair left. Have you noticed how geese are silent the whole time they're floating around? And they make no noise while waddling, scavenging the lake shore in search of edible vegetation. But when it's time to take off or land, you better be ready for some real-time racket. They are uproarious on arrival and departure. It's as if they are saying to onlookers, *hey look at us, we are a spectacle to behold*. Mom says she thinks it's the male and female geese arguing over directions. The males with their lower honking are crying out, "left, left, left". And the females in their higher pitch are calling "right, right, right!" I'm not sure she's correct on that one. I prefer to think the geese don't have much need to argue. They seem happy just being who they are like the kid I saw at the bowling alley.

SECRETS OF PIANO MOVERS—SARAH

This has been the week of the earache. Monday night, just as I was getting ready to set up the mannequin in the window and slip out to work, Clarence awoke, moaning. That's the best way to describe it. I was in my grey sweats — my church cleaning outfit — and when I went in his room, he gave me a strange look but then just started pulling on his earlobe. He said it was killing him. He said it felt like someone had taken a needle and poked it in his ear. Then he rolled back on his side and cupped the ear in his hand. I got a warm cloth and some aspirin and sat on the side of his bed, nestled his ear in the cloth, until he could finally fall asleep. I had to rush to do the cleaning; I just skipped the mopping because the floor looked okay.

Clarence woke up again at 7:00 and said it was even worse, not a needle this time but an ice pick. So, we went to Med Express. Well, that was quite the taxing experience. You'd think they'd have our information saved since that's where I've taken him for school checkups, but they once again had to ask us a litany of questions: Is there any history of cancer in your family? Of heart disease? Has he ever broken a bone? I felt like yelling at the top of my lungs: "he has swimmer's ear and needs antibiotics", but I just kept my cool, figuring that would be the best path toward having him feeling better. They prescribed ear drops that, when I went to CVS, they said would cost $345.00 without insurance. It's hard to believe that something in such a small bottle, that is mostly water, can cost so much. But I knew he needed it, or his earache would just get worse. So, I put it on the credit card. Still, it took four full days for him to start feeling better. *An earache can really throw you*, he said when he was finally feeling better. It makes you forget who you are.

Everyone has a secret life, Francie Noland establishes in that classic children's book *A Tree Grows in Brooklyn*. Now that's a lozenge which softens and melts in the mouth. We do all have a life on the outside which we allow others to see, and then we have the inner life that only we ourselves know. Keeping the two in balance is as precarious a business as moving a piano. Both can lose equilibrium in a heartbeat without proper handling, without the kid glove treatment. Balancing the secret inner life and the public outer life resembles correctly moving a piano.

Sometimes I think of myths and fables as excellent compromise points between fact and fiction. If you consider it carefully, myths are real if you allow your mind to work that way. I mean, they portray reality and teach vital lessons. So, is that any less significant than some kind of quantifiable truth? I heard of an American Indian storyteller who would introduce stories saying, "I don't know if this story happened. But I know it is true."

Aesop's are my favorite fables. Remember *The Dog and His Reflection*? In case you don't, there's this dog who thinks the bone in his lake's water reflection is bigger than the bone he is carrying in his mouth. So, he opens his mouth and drops his bone. He loses the actual bone because he sees one that looks more appealing. Now, that's an excellent way to teach the dangers of wanting and striving for more than what you need. Similarly, *The Town Mouse and The Country Mouse* affirms the wisdom of depending on the earth's provisions. The country mouse, who seems so disheveled and poor, is actually the one to triumph. His satisfaction with simple pleasures offers him a security the city mouse can never enjoy.

Yesterday on the interstate I passed a tractor trailer carrying cows. The enormous eyes of two of them peering through the metal bars just about made my heart sink. I told myself at least they didn't know where they were going. But maybe that's merely a myth — a fable — I tell myself to stay afloat. Maybe they knew exactly what they were destined for. This reminds me of a poem I love. It's by Jane Mead:

Passing a Truck Full of Chickens at Night on Highway Eighty
What struck me first was their panic.
Some were pulled by the wind from moving to the ends of the stacked cages,
some had their heads blown through the bars — and could not get them in again.

Some hung there like that – dead – their own feathers blowing, clotting in
their faces. Then
I saw the one that made me slow some –
I lingered there beside her for five miles.
She had pushed her head through the space between bars – to get a better
view.
She had the look of a dog in the back of a pickup, that eager look of a dog
who knows she's being taken along.
She craned her neck.
She looked around, watched me, then strained to see over the car – strained
to see what happened beyond.
That is the chicken I want to be.

What a triumphant ending that poem has! Jane Mead could unveil glory amid a seemingly tragic scenario. That's what I hope to do in this life: to show Clarence and show myself—show the world—that mystery, beauty, love, and glory will arrive just when you least expect them and in the unlikeliest of places. That's the whole story of Christmas, after all: the unwed mother, the inept Joseph, the meager manger, the shepherds shocked by celestial messengers, the magi striking out on a journey at the sight of a star, a tiny baby born to bring peace to the world.

But then there are also stories that seem to be the opposite of glory and triumph. There's one I can't get out of my head. Two Novembers ago a local family—mother, father, two kids, and a private pilot—got caught in a frozen rainstorm. The plane's wings became weighed down with ice, and they literally fell from the sky. The plane just fell from the sky. How long did they know they would die? Did the mother sing to her children at the end? Did they just pass out from the speed and force of falling? These things we will never know. It's almost too much to think of, too hard to imagine what they must have gone through.

SECOND LETTER FROM PETER—CLARENCE

Did you know that the word talent used to mean money? I'm talking about a long time ago, but it's true. I can see how this works because talent is like a hidden treasure chest, something of value you own—like my word collection. And what's even better is that talent doesn't get spent, doesn't get used up. But then if you don't spend it or use it, you lose it.

Mom has explained to me many times that I am an exceptional—her word—child, talented at particular things and that my memory for numbers and patterns and details is super-duper good. She says this is true of kids with Asperger's. So, I figure I'm lucky to be this way, to be what I heard her tell my teacher once, "on the spectrum". I know that she's talking about the spectrum of autism, but just saying on the spectrum makes it sound like I'm part of a rainbow. I'd probably be the red stripe, if I had a choice in these matters.

I got a second letter from Peter, which arrived on a Wednesday exactly ten days after I'd sent mine. It was raining, so I tucked the letter under my shirt until I got back in the apartment.

Dear Clarence,

Thank you for your letter. I'll start by answering your questions. I don't have any kids. Linus is like a kid to me though. I teach writing at St. Louis Community College. I'm impressed with how well you write.

I know City Museum. Did you venture out on the bus they've got suspended from the roof? I look at it sometimes from the street when I'm running errands and think it would take a brave soul to go in there.

Sorry to hear your backpack is so cumbersome. I remember that from when I was in middle school, lugging such a heavy thing around.

Do you like sports? I'm an enormous baseball fan. I used to play catcher and can't seem to get over my passion for the sport. The Cardinals are my favorite team. Maybe we could watch a game together some day. I'll get this in the mail to you. It's almost 4:00 in the afternoon, the time the letters go out.

Your pen pal,
Peter

COME WHAT MAY—SARAH

Most of what I do seems to get undone. I suspect this to be true for plenty of people. But it has struck me recently that the toilet I clean and the floor I mop will, if things go well — if people keep on coming to church — return to their dirty state within a few days. And at home it's true, too. Come to think of it, so much of life is like that. I wonder if the girl at Hair Cuttery who trimmed my hair today secretly hopes it will grow back quickly, so she has to redo the cutting; or if she hopes her work will hold and I won't need to darken their door again. Repeatedly redoing what becomes undone is the source of job security. And maybe it is the source of meaning and joy in life.

And this makes me wonder how you know when the perfect time is for anything. There are so many things we cannot — and should not — know as we are doing and redoing things in our lives. That's why being a parent is so frightening. How do you know what you are doing, and when you are doing it is right? This indelible story parents are writing without knowing it could be all wrong. And we'll never know until our children are all the way grown. And maybe not even then.

When Clarence was still an infant, around 18 months, and I needed to put him in the Pack and Play to get something done, he would unfailingly throw all the animals out of the playpen and then scream at the top of his lungs. I would return to him, pick up the toys and hand them to him, wanting to assure him he was cared for. But what I wonder now is if I was just encouraging the habit of throwing a tantrum. And there are much bigger examples of uncertainty in parenting, like the fact that I am keeping a secret from him, a secret he deserves to know.

There are truly more unknowns in the world than we care to admit. But there is one thing I am certain about. Clarence and I talked about it yesterday. If a restaurant shows pictures — photographs of what your meal will look like — on its front window, that's a pretty clear sign you should not eat at that restaurant. At least this is clear and helps you make one correct decision in life.

Last week I took Clarence to the movies, and we played our usual game of rating the previews. I believe I enjoy that more than the movie itself. It's strange how you can be closer to a person, sometimes, when you are sitting beside them than when you are facing each other. Maybe it's something about looking at the same thing and recognizing you both must be feeling something similar, like when you sit on the beach beside a friend and look out at the same sunrise over the calm, blue morning water. It's like you are closer that way than at any other time. Maybe people sitting together in church experience something similar, focused as they are on the sacred.

Clarence and I have made a God Exists list. On it we note occurrences that help undergird, or at least sustain, what belief we may have. I hope it might remind us of light when there is true darkness, hope when there is despair, joy when there is sadness, and love as it seems so frequently absent in our world. Usually the entries, our observations, are small and unremarkable. Like the fact that I'm looking for my glasses, and at the very moment when I panic that I've lost them, there they are right in the fold of the bedspread. Or on a walk in the early summer I see my first cornflower of the year. I love their raggedness and their perfect periwinkle color. I also love that it's called chicory. That a noble word, chicory. But that such beauty and color will grow untended and wild on the side of the road is, to me, proof that God exists. I've posted the list on the refrigerator and try not to rush over when Clarence adds to it. But I feel like I recalibrate when he does, for something inside of me resets to where it should be. Last week he wrote: Josh and Adam asked me to play in their foursquare game at recess.

Some religions believe that God is inside of each of us, that God is present and manifested in our best selves. That thought brings me peace. It's a dizzying peace, the kind you get after being twisted on a swing, twisted and twisted until the swing unwinds and you try to walk and nearly fall down. You forget yourself for that moment. More than anything, I remember best how things felt rather than how they looked. I am not as good as my mother was at rattling off statistics, but I can tell you pretty precisely how something tasted, or how it was shaped, or how it exuded a kind of warmth. Maybe that's what God is, a roadmap to help us understand how things felt and so how they truly are. I have the sneaking sensation we all think about this a lot whether we want to admit it — even to ourselves — or not, and especially whether we talk to others about it. Imagination is just how we interpret what we encounter. Maybe that's what God is: living imagination.

Speaking of imagination, last spring Clarence played baseball with the Rolla Little League. It took a good bit of imagination for me to envision him on a baseball team. But Clarence said he had baseball on the mind. That's how he put it. *I've got baseball on the mind and want to give it a go.* He said he had a new friend who loved it and he suspected he might too. At first, I did my best to discourage him because all I could see was Clarence sitting in the dugout the entire time. But because he mentioned a friend, I agreed. And I was impressed with how fair the coaches were and how they seemed eager to include him. He played right outfielder and spent much of the time just standing. He never really caught on to the "keep-on-moving" advice. But I am sure it was good for him, good to be part of a group. Sitting in the bleachers, watching his games, I felt proud of him, proud that he was just out there. But I could not get over how sometimes the umpires in Clarence's baseball games made such ludicrous calls. Did they really not see what happened? Maybe they were going with their imaginations. And there's nothing we can do about it.

WHISPERING IS LOUDER THAN TALKING—
CLARENCE

When people whisper a secret, a sudden quiet descends as everyone nearby cranes their necks and strains their ears to hear what's being said. And in places where you are meant to be quiet—the doctor's waiting room, during a fire drill at school, or at the movies—if someone ends up talking it is really startling, almost like they are shouting. So, if you think of it, whispering is louder than talking. It's loud in the sense that it holds more weight. Whispering has influence and sway.

Saturdays I'm home, and Mom's at the Y doing her front desk job. Also, on Thursdays she has to be at work until 8:00 at night. As far as snacks go, I have four options. The first is cereal, which I eat right out of the box. Why bother with a bowl when you can dig your hand in and instantly touch what will taste sweet? The second option is ramen. Mom says it's okay if I heat water, but only in the microwave, flat out no using the stove when I'm alone. I pour the boiling water over the ramen noodles, then dump in the mysterious contents of the flavor packet. Pretty sure bet it's unhealthy. But it's good, so who cares? The third food offsets the ramen: carrots, which are good for your eyesight. And the fourth is a sandwich. My favorite is white bread, salami, and pepperoni—that's it. No mayonnaise, no lettuce, no mustard, no nothing.

After that, if the weather's okay, I bounce my basketball in the empty parking spaces right out front of our apartment building. I'm perfecting my dribbling. Next winter I plan to play on the U13 team at the Y. If it's too cold or rainy, I head on over to Rent-To-Own secretly hoping Larry's there. Today it looks like he's not. When I peered in, I couldn't see him. But I noticed that in the Big O of the store's sign a pigeon had taken up residence, perched there as if it was meant for him exclusively. I enjoy thinking about that: a pigeon perched in Rent-to-Own's Letter O.

Because of that, I go on in. Maybe Larry will be in the back. Maybe he will be there after all. And he is — right in the back, putting together cardboard boxes. He says he'll need them when things get busy, when the students leave come summer. After we do that for a while, Larry sits down in the chair next to my La-Z-Boy and we just shoot the breeze for a while. He doesn't ask me the usual questions adults drill you with. He doesn't ask about school or what hobbies I may have. It's like he's ok being together looking at the TV. Maybe he's already picked up on the fact that it is just Mom and me living next door. But I like it that he talks to me and not at me, not like I am just some kid he's trying to please or teach a lesson to.

I decide to let him in on one of my secrets. I tell him all about the balloon releasing project. And he is really interested, says it's amazing that one went all the way to St. Louis. He says when he was a kid he would let balloons go too. He nods when I tell him about my balloon project, or about Peaches' bird gaping. He nods like he gets what I'm saying, like he gets how I feel. Things change in him, though, when I tell him about Fred the foldable man, Mom's collapsible mannequin. Suddenly it seems like he wants to talk about something else. He says we should go put together more boxes.

Back in the apartment, I fiddle around with the Newton's Cradle I got last Christmas. In case you've never seen one, these devices are made up of five steel balls each the size of a nickel which hang on pieces of fishing line. Picture a miniature swing-set. When you pull one marble out sideways and let it fall, the balls bang against one another — tick, tick, tick. I love the sound of it, and that they all move together. It's a kind of magic trick. Sir Isaac Newton invented it to teach about momentum. I find it strange that some people get to have "sir" before their name: Sir Clarence, Sir Evan, Sir Harry, Sir Isaac Newton.

I've been thinking that in life you are not hiding if people know where you are. Also, if no one cares where you are, you aren't really hiding either. But what about hiding from yourself? What about hiding parts of yourself from yourself? That seems like something we all do in some fashion or another. I do. And I feel there's a lot Mom is hiding from both herself and from me, maybe more from herself than from me.

YOU'RE OKAY—SARAH

Once I am sure Clarence is asleep and before I get dressed to go into work, I listen to the sounds of our apartment. Around ten p.m. the world's quietness amplifies otherwise unnoticed noises. In the distance, you can hear the moan of trucks on highway 63, the occasional high pitch of a jake brake. Closer in, a car door shuts, and the wheels of a trash can rumble as it is rolled out to the street. Inside the apartment, the heat kicks on, a sound that never ceases to soothe me. Sometimes I stand outside Clarence's room and listen for the soft sweet sounds he sometimes makes when asleep. This is one of my favorite times of day, the lull of it all, the sense of enclosure.

Long before I met Henry, I thought it possible to be most anything in the world. All you had to do was set your mind to it. And I'd like Clarence to grow up believing this too. Maybe that's the actual reason I've kept so much from him. I want him to see possibilities, not consequences. Let me give you an image. The summer before my senior year, I went up to Saratoga Springs, New York to look at Skidmore College. It was August, and so that town was in full horse racing mode. So, we went, one afternoon, to the flat track. We ended up near the paddock where jockeys mount. And Angel Cordero, a man the size of a child, stood before this enormous three-year-old racehorse he was about to mount. He stood in front of that wild-eyed stallion and kissed him in the center of a blaze on his nose. He wasn't thinking of how, in moments, he'd be saddled on that colossal animal running around a track at 38 miles an hour. Cordero was filled with possibilities. He was thinking he would win. It was magnificent. And win he did. Yes, he did.

Have you ever bumped into someone at Walmart, or become caught up in staring at stamps under glass at the post office and failed to notice the line you are waiting in had moved forward? You're so clearly in the way, blocking or hindering someone else, but when you say excuse me, the person responds you're okay. I love that. All day you've been cataloguing the ways you've fallen short and then some stranger tells you you're okay. It's incredibly uplifting if you think about it, permitting others to simply be themselves in their space. It was the opposite with Henry, who always saw something as missing or wrong with me. When with him it was like I was perpetually playing pin the tail on the donkey. I was blindfolded and expected to pin the tail in the right spot. But I was always off target.

Attention K-mart Shoppers. We have a blue light special. The world constantly demands our attention. It seems to want us distracted, wants us looking hither and thither. Wants us to leave our space or be and act differently in our space. And it is all so jarring. Our modern world is noisy. Think of all the things that do this: our computer updates need loading, the water filter changing, the telemarketer is calling. Your cellphone chirps, your car beeps, the tea pot whistles. Nothing is quiet. Even once a store's got you in the building, they still demand our attention. It's disconcerting, the opposite of peaceful, grounded, purposeful. And if you think about it hard enough, it is the opposite of mercy, a word that once meant pity and thanks. Ever since I met a majestic Great Pyrenees named Mercy, I've had an image for the word. Mercy is a gigantic white dog with a tendency to wander who exudes nothing but sweetness and gentleness. That is Mercy. Remember, as a kid twisting your friend's arm until she called out "mercy, mercy"? It was a game. You'd twist hard, stay at it until your friend yelled "mercy". And that's what made you stop. Mercy is the word I think of when I worry Clarence will wonder why I sleep late and am tired during the day. I don't want him to suspect there's something wrong with me, that I drink at night or am really depressed. It's mercy that I rely upon to let Clarence have ease with our lives as they are — at least for now.

PUBLIC SERVICE ANNOUNCEMENT—CLARENCE

This is random, but I think being alive is actually a lot like playing the game of tetherball. In case you are rusty on this playground game, it is rather simple. There's a steel pole secured into the ground; the pole is a little thinner and much shorter than a flagpole. Then there's a volleyball tied to a string. Two people play, and the goal is to wind the ball around the pole in the direction you are facing while your opponent is trying to wind the ball around the pole in the opposite direction. And this is like life because sometimes when you do something, you're on a roll, heading in the right direction, winding the ball around the pole and then—bang—someone comes along and undoes everything you accomplished, in one fell swoop. And you just have to keep on trying, hitting the ball again, trying again, until it's winding in your direction once more. I tell you this as a kind of public service announcement, so you will know. This is one reason I eat different kinds of cereal. You never can be sure which one will make you strong. Think about how Popeye found that spinach gave him strength. You can find what you need in the least expected of places is what I sometimes think.

THE FIRST INVISIBLE THING—SARAH

There are no words for it, really. That's what Clarence said yesterday when I came into the kitchen. He was working on his owl, sitting at the kitchen table pasting shreds of yesterday's sports page on the bird's back. He was so engrossed in what he was doing and thinking he didn't even look up when I entered the room. *No words for what?* I thought. I poured myself a cup of the morning's lukewarm coffee and sat down in the chair opposite him and chimed in, *I know what you mean, sometimes there are not words.* This is when he looked up and listed what was on his mind: *altitude, oxygen, helium, pressure, distance, fear, loneliness, and anger. Invisible things,* he said; *that is my list of invisible things.* He said it with such pride in his voice, as if he'd finally figured out the solution to a worldwide problem.

To parse out how Clarence sees the world would be one astounding feat. But I've learned over the years not to trespass too much on his musings. I've learned that the best thing to do is to join him when he thinks aloud like this. So, I asked him what he believed the first ever invisible thing might have been. And he looked me in the eye and answered *cats, I think cats.* Well, that threw me for a loop. But I sort of get it. Cats are there, and then they are not. They slink out of sight— gone. Maybe he's imagining how a cat might never come back, might run away and be invisible. Then, after a lengthy pause he looked at me again and said, *No, the first invisible thing was a spider web, definitely a spider web because they are invisible until water gets on them. And then they turn into sparkling jewel necklaces. It's not until light hits a wet spider web that you can see it. Isn't that amazing, Mom?* All I could think was how amazing it was that he thought of that, that he noticed it in the first place.

THE DISAPPEARANCE OF SEE-SAWS—CLARENCE

I like the way branches throw shadows inside buildings on winter mornings. At 10:31 on Friday, the shadow of the tree outside our classroom window fell directly across my desk. We were in Language Arts. We were diagramming sentences, and my desk branch looked exactly like what Mr. Abel wanted us to copy from the whiteboard into our composition books. When I wrote *slowly* on the adverb line under *running* on the verb line, I tried to make the letters teeny tiny, each one a miniature bird perched on a branch.

In math class we had a carnival. This will take some explaining. We were all assigned to teams of three and had to come up with a game that exhibited our mastery of a particular math concept that we'd covered in the past month. Sam, Evan and I had three ping-pong balls. When you came to our station, you had to guess how many balls would go into three cups over the course of five throws. Mrs. Murphy had brought in a snow cone maker, like a home version of one, and we ate cone after cone of overly sweet blue ice. When we visited other groups' stations, we put up a sign we'd made that read **Sorry-we are closed. Will be back in five to ten minutes**. It made the entire thing seem extremely official. I loved that about it.

Across the parking lot from Henley Middle School is Brownsville Elementary. Yesterday during his recess, a third grader climbed all the way to the top of a tree on the Brownsville playground. No one seemed to notice. The teachers were all talking with each other in a group, looking down at their feet and occasionally gesturing. And this kid just kept on climbing up and up and up. We were outside in PE playing kick the can, and I saw the kid climbing the tree from where I was stuck in jail. So up goes the kid. At first, he looks kind of euphoric, like he's accomplished an astounding feat. But soon you can tell he's really and truly stuck. Finally, the teachers notice. They walk over to the tree and call to him: *Ryan, Ryan come down.* They try to coax him down by telling him there's a branch just a few inches below his sneaker. But by now Ryan's visibly terrified. He is not moving one bit. It took a while, but eventually a fire truck came to get him out of the tree. The truck had on its lights and everything. I would like to congratulate that kid Ryan, ask him what he saw from his high perch. I want to tell him he's a talented tree climber.

Since we're discussing playgrounds, let's turn our attention to the see-saw. Have you noticed how rare they are? Mom says she used to play on them with her best friend all the time. She'd trap Louisa up in the air and ask her questions she wouldn't dare ask otherwise in actual life. Then Louisa would do the same thing to Mom. She'd ask her if she'd rather have a hamster or a ferret — which was a tender question for Mom whose parents let her have no pets, not even a goldfish. No pets for my mom. Ever. All her childhood she wanted a cat so badly she told me she felt like she would combust from all the wanting. Me: I have an actual fish tank, and Peaches. It's a sweet and sour relationship. I'll tell you why later on.

But let's get back to the subject of see-saws. It was like Mom and her best friend allowed each other to dream of things out loud as they were suspended up in the air, tethered to the earth only by one another's legs. I bet there's some rule now that says playgrounds can't have seesaws. I just bet there's a regulation proclaiming them to be unsafe. And I'm figuring that after the Ryan-tree incident there will now be a rule that says kids are not allowed to climb trees on the playground. It makes me sad how we have tried to make the world so safe when it's really so much less safe in the most important ways.

SPONTANEOUS COMBUSTION—SARAH

If you bale hay before it is dry all the way, fermentation will occur. This can cause spontaneous combustion. I know because I saw it happen when I was ten at summer camp. We were all at dinner in the cafeteria when the huge camp bell rang, and we were told the barn was on fire. Our counselors instructed us to run as quickly as we could, all of us, down to the lake and to fill buckets with water. We made an assembly line and passed the buckets one by one. Then we watched as the counselors led all the horses—which they had blindfolded with leg wraps—out to safety in the pasture. They had to blindfold the horses because they would have stood stock still, refused to move when they saw fire. It was otherworldly watching these colossal beasts being led blindly out of a burning barn.

There's the technical, actual kind of spontaneous combustion, which I have just described, and then there are the times when you feel yourself about to burst into flame. You believe it possible that you will simply catch on fire, unannounced. At least I do. This is a sensation I have more often that I'd like to admit. I fear I will just go up in smoke— poof. And it's not only as an adult that I have felt this way. I remember as a kid thinking I might change into something else. It was, and still is, one of the more unsettling feelings, as you can imagine. It's why I don't mind this job I have cleaning the church. I have an actual task I need to complete. It is a straightforward task, and when it's done, I'm done. If I've mopped the kitchen with Spic & Span (whoever came up with that name should earn a prize); mopped it as well as I can, there's little more I can do. It is clean, done, nothing to change for the time being. And that is an agreeable feeling. I know I will not become or turn into anything else, at least for the time being.

In my early twenties, I found out that in the very quarry to whose waters I'd jumped, a girl my age drowned the following week. A power line that had come down in a storm electrocuted her. It's true, but strange, that things of different levels of seriousness can occupy the same space in your heart's memory. The same is true with my about-to-combust feeling.

THE PRICE IS RIGHT—CLARENCE

Until last week, I'd never invited a friend over to our apartment. I guess I'd been afraid he'd find it strange how we live in a strip mall, wedged between Rent-To-Own and Mabel's Marvelous Manicures (and the owner's name is not even Mabel). But ever since Evan told me his dad works until six, and he's home alone every afternoon, I figured we could hang out together on Wednesday. Mom said it would be fine, just reminded me about no stove usage. She said she'd drive him home once she got off work.

After chowing down on Lucky Charms, we headed on over to Rent-to-Own so Evan could see for himself what I'd told him about the place. Well, not only was the popcorn maker full with a freshly filled stack of bags beside it, but Larry visited with us in the Lazy-Z-Boys and handed us each a coke. We'd plopped ourselves down in front of the wide screen and were watching *The Price Is Right* when Larry walked over and said, *You boys look mighty thirsty; here you go.*

It surprised me to discover that Evan likes *The Price Is Right* as much as I do. Truth be told, I didn't think most kids had even heard of the show. I'd planned on keeping my liking it to myself, but when we flipped through the channels, I had to pause at least a moment at *The Price is Right* to see what item was up for guessing its price. And Evan immediately blurted out: $245.00 for the deep freezer. So, I just stopped flipping, and we watched. And lo-and-behold, the correct price was $230.50. I gave him a high five. Next up was an entire bedroom. It looked so weird to see a dresser, a mirror, a bed, and reading chair all arranged there on the stage as if it was really in someone's home. The bedroom set—that's what they called it—went for $875.00. My guess was way off, like $200.00 under the actual price. I guess those bedroom getups are real popular.

After *The Price Is Right*, we went back to the apartment. I was thinking about letting Evan have a peek at Foldable Fred but then decided against it. It might throw things off kilter and be awkward. So, we made ramen and talked about this kid who made the entire Taj Mahal out of Legos. He told us about it on Monday on our way to lunch. I still haven't found the right way to ask him how he did it because it might seem like I am planning on copying his idea. Plus, what I want is an answer other than the one I think I'll get. What I'm afraid he'll say is *I followed the directions*. Directions are far more complicated than actual tasks. Directions chop things up into way too many steps.

Here's an example of the dangers of directions: on the back of last week's cereal box was a paint-by-number picture of a parrot. Because Mom was still asleep, and I'd run out of things to do, I pulled the liner bag out of the cereal box, cut around the parrot oh so carefully, and dug in the kitchen drawer until I found four different colored markers. I filled in the yellows first, like the directions said. They were marked number one. But, horrifically, the bird looked like it was cold. Then I colored the number two spaces red—like the directions said—and the parrot looked like it was both cold and bleeding. So, I just colored the whole bird black and made it into a crow. A crow is a whole lot better than a cold, bleeding parrot, if you ask me. Directions give the illusion of control. And we're vulnerable beings, subject to the weather and time; we are tiny boats that get sloshed about whenever the slightest wave comes along.

THERE'S MORE TO ALL THIS THAN WE THOUGHT— SARAH

Every story begins somewhere. Now that I have shown Clarence the mannequin, the story of it has begun for him. And there's no telling how it will end. I am certain that for the time being I cannot tell him that this very thing was perched in a chair in his father's office for four days during exams to make it look like someone was holding office hours when he'd left the university, left the state, flew the coop to be with his graduate student lover.

Stage magicians talk to keep the audience from seeing what they are doing. They ask questions to distract people, or they talk about the weather or the traffic. Meanwhile, they are busy switching out a playing card or stuffing a hankie up a sleeve, hiding a rabbit in a hat. And, in a way, we all do this. Especially parents. Particularly mothers. I am all the time trying to steer Clarence away from asking too much about who his father is and why he's not around. Yesterday, when I suspected he was about to ask, I explained the phenomenon of pet rocks. These were all the rage when I was in middle school. Now just take a moment to think about it and only it: pet rocks. A rock that is a pet. Pet rocks. Wild! And people got serious about them, named them and clothed them, the whole nine yards.

This one kid, Dan, who was in my seventh-grade class, even had a grass floored hut for his pet rock, Omi, whose eyes were those plastic googly eyes. Omi was painted a dark, dark green. But here's the thing: his affection for his rock stopped being funny when Dan's mom was thrown by her horse and went into a coma from a head injury. The class brought little trinkets for Dan's Omi, and it turned out to be a magnificent way to show our sympathy. So maybe there's more to all this than we thought. Maybe pet rocks, and other seemingly frivolous articles, are crucial.

When I lived in Washington, DC working as an intern, most Saturdays I would take the bus out Constitution Avenue to wander around Rock Creek Cemetery which is one of the oldest in the city. It's where members of many prestigious Washington families are buried. And each time I went, I stood before the statue called Grief. It's by Augustus Saint-Gaudens. The writer Henry Adams commissioned it after his wife, Clover, a photographer, drank citric acid stop bath and killed herself. Adams told Saint-Gaudens that he wanted an androgynous piece to be their shared gravestone upon his death. Reading up on the entire story, I discovered that after Clover died Adams destroyed every single photograph she had ever taken. He ripped them up one by one into teeny tiny pieces. He refused to ever speak of her again. That story sticks with me for sure. Maybe Dan's pet rock was like the statue Grief. Maybe it became his Grief, this rock, with its soft grassy place to live and teeny tiny plastic grapes and miniature beach balls that his classmates have given to him.

IT MATTERS HOW YOU TELL THE STORY—
CLARENCE

When you tell a story, grab your audience's attention. Leave in the important details and let the other ones go. Personally, during bowling, I like to make a name for myself—a name that is definitely not my own, like Dylan or Tyler. I do this because it makes me feel something exhilarating when DYLAN shows up in bright lights on the electronic scoreboard. I am someone else—it says it right there in neon—for a full 45 minutes, sometimes more. Plus, I like the fact that the room is dimly lit and there's even a disco reflection ball making triples of everything on the ceiling. To be Dylan under disco lights seems just about right. So, I'd leave all that in if I told a bowling story. That would be important.

Did you know that seven-eighths of an iceberg is actually under water? That means we only see one-eighth of it. Our teacher said that Ernest Hemingway—this guy who wrote about war, hated adjectives, and drank lots of martinis—used the iceberg image to warn want-to-be writers not to tell everything they know in a story. Like an iceberg, he advised, it's an excellent practice to leave the better part of what you have to say submerged. And I fully agree with that dude, Hemingway. I also think this can be the same with people. If you find out everything about a person the first time you hang out together, there's not much left to discover. But sometimes what is submerged and hidden is what can really hurt. Think of the ship, the Titanic, that was ripped open below the waterline. Sometimes I feel like I am cut or poked really badly by what I cannot see. Sometimes I feel stung by the world with no warning.

Why in the world do people ask what a book is about? If you can sum up a book in simple conversation, then why read it in the first place? And why write the book if you can tell what it means with a few sentences. A superb book is an entire other life that you carry around with you and refer back to, particularly when the going gets rough. You can live pretty much full time in a book if the need arises. That is what Mom says.

My new strategy, when asked this book question, is to summarize the plot in one overly simple sentence. Yesterday a tall lady at the "Y" — where I was sitting on the bench waiting for Mom to get off work — asked what *Of Mice and Men* was about when she saw me reading it. I told her it's about an oversized kid who doesn't mean to hurt small things, but does, and really regrets it afterwards. Now that doesn't sound super exciting, does it? But when you meet Lennie and see him crying over that dead mouse, you feel things you haven't felt before in your entire life. And when he kills the girl but doesn't mean to, and his best friend has to shoot him, you are never the same again.

Your dad would have been mighty proud of you, the tall "Y" lady said. That's when everything went bright white in my head. My dad? She looked half through me and said *I'm sorry, I must have been thinking of someone else.* Then she started digging around in her purse to make it look like she was urgently searching for keys or glasses. It's the opposite of how magicians talk about unnecessary things to hide what they are really doing. This lady was doing something unnecessary to avoid talking. So, I walked away slowly, my head spinning.

Mom reads books like it's going out of style. I sometimes end up asking her what a book is about, even though I know in reality it makes no sense to do that. But it's my best strategy to find out what's on her mind. Usually she shares some cool quotes. The book she's reading right now is called *Why Be Happy When You Can Be Normal*. Now that's a title that catches you off guard. Here's the quote she chose: *my mother was out of scale, larger than life. She was like a fairytale story where size is approximate and unstable.* After she read that quote, she set down her book, and we talked about it for a while. She explained that approximate meant relative to things around it, not exactly the same. So, the writer's mother in Mom's book is sometimes huge. Other times, not so much. It's like how things sometimes appear different in dreams. At the end of our mini pow wow, Mom told me to always trust my heart. She said the one time she completely followed her heart it ended up with an excellent product: me.

My favorite little kid book is *Ferdinand the Bull*. I love the way the bull's mother lets him sit under the cork tree and smell the flowers. He is perfectly content being just who he is. Not even the bullfighters — who use pins and bright red to get him all revved up — can keep Ferdinand from what he loves, sitting under that tree quietly. Mom used to read it to me, and as soon as she read the ending: *I bet he's still smelling the flowers*, I asked her to read it again. *Again*, I'd say, *again*. And most often she did.

There's a famous book called *The Adventures of Huckleberry Finn* that takes place right here in Missouri. The kid Huck spends time on the Mississippi River. When he and his friend, Tom, run away, all the people think Huck is dead when really, he's not. So, they have a funeral for him, and he goes to it. He watches his own funeral! It is not really his funeral, but everyone thinks it is. What a wild experience that would be. First off, you'd get to hear what people really and truly think of you, like deep down think of you. And second, you'd find out who overeats by watching who shovels down too much food at the reception. We all know that one of the principal reasons for the gathering after a funeral service is to eat enough so you sort of prove to yourself that you're not the one lying in the casket. At my grandmother's funeral there were ham biscuits, and I ate twelve of them. They were the little kind, but still, twelve is a lot. I'm secretly proud.

The guy who wrote *The Adventures of Huckleberry Finn* has an entire forest named after him. Last April, during spring break, Mom and I went to Mark Twain National Forest, which is about an hour from Rolla. She sat under a tree — sort of like Ferdinand — and read beside the river while I scavenged for good skipping stones. I made a gigantic pile and worked on my skill. The highest number I got was 16, but you should have seen the first eight or nine water strikes as the perfectly flat stone skated over the water. After that I just plopped myself down and stared into the river. I love to watch fish swimming, the way they move, their shadows between the rocks. It amazes me how they can breathe in the water. Logically I get it, but when I really think about it, think about how they are breathing through their gills, it makes me jiggle inside.

I hate it when someone asks how my day or weekend was. Well, a day is a long time. A lot can happen. Some of it is good and some of it not so much. It's nearly impossible to recap the entire thing. Also, it's cumbersome when school starts in the fall, and your new teacher asks what you did over the summer. What did I do this summer? Well, let me think, do you have a week for me to give you a summary of that? Mom and I have this game to tell about our days. It's called ten: top ten things you saw today, ten most outrageous things teachers said, ten low points of the day. Our numbering is random, and we both usually end up keeling over in laughter. Here are a few examples of top and bottom things.

Mom's tops: watching a bird carry scraps of yarn to its nest, going back and forth from the yarn source — which is usually a dumpster — to the nest; hearing a tiny kid singing to himself while walking home from school; the smell of rain on streets in summer.

Mom's lows: fire drill at the Y while meditating in yoga class, ice on the windshield in the mornings, surprises.

My tops: figuring out how to chew gum in class without getting caught; feeding the mouse that lives in my locker at school; getting chosen to do the morning announcements on the PA system.

My lows: the substitute bus driver I'll tell you about later; indoor recess; keyboarding class.

UNIVERSAL LOST AND FOUND—SARAH

Clarence told me of an idea he has for a universal lost and found. It would be a place where objects people have lost—a scarf, a coin purse, a hubcap—are kept safe and sound until reclaimed. He explained this idea in such exquisite detail I could envision this place: walls of a soft color; old wooden floor with dips where people walking on it have worn spots thin. Those in charge of tending to the Lost and Found would take great pride in their job, be ever on alert and hopeful that an object and its rightful owner might become reunited under their watch. If there were one, I'd take the necklace I found at church there. Still don't know why I took it home. But now it's too late to take it back.

Then we talked about how we sometimes want to hide, but part of us wants to be found, while another part of us wants to remain hidden, stay just out of reach. The Beatles wrote about it in Octopus' Garden: *We would sing and dance around because we know we can't be found. I'd like to be under the sea in an octopus' garden in the shade.* Maybe that is the greatest riddle in life: we want to be found—but on our own terms.

There is a yellow tray I keep on our kitchen table. On it is the image of a red and orange butterfly. Some days I put a small leaf on the tray for her to eat, but she doesn't seem to notice. She never eats it, even though I sometimes pretend she does. I love this tray. My first boyfriend gave it to me. We were in our early twenties, living in Vermont on land his family owned. He was a biathlete, cross county skied 26 miles at top speed with a seven-pound rifle on his back. Every two miles, he had to bring his heart rate down to shoot at a target set up on the course. He would aim his rifle at the bull's-eye, pull the trigger, then ski off at top speed without even checking his points. When he came upon the next target, he would do the same thing over again.

We lived in a greenhouse we'd built together, just the two of us. We heated it with a Tululeke wood stove made of soapstone and held the heat so well. In late January, we started the tomato saplings that were our bread and butter, and we had the first tomatoes in the state of Vermont, sold them come April at Brattleboro Farmer's Market. During the night in the greenhouse we had to stoke the stove every five hours to keep it going.

Michael had gorgeous hands and a sweet, round face. It was as if we were stand-ins, living a life we both recognized we couldn't sustain. I knew that as the years swept by, I would grow tired of living this life of seclusion, away from people, away from books and schools. But it remains a lit room in my mind, those months we ran that tomato farm. When I remember it all now, I see that greenhouse we were living in, remember how it was a translucent semi-circle open to the stars and the sky. The days held a luster I have yet to replicate. I looked Michael up on the internet the other day and found out he's still running the farm — with a wife and two blond Norwegian looking children, a girl and a boy.

Saturday nights, Michael would go visit his grandmother, Lodi. She was the tiniest adult I have ever seen. She imitated a rooster's call — kickereekee — in the most captivating way when she told stories of them roosting on her thatched roof in Nordhausen when she was a child. Michael would turn on her kitchen radio, and they would waltz to whatever classical music he could find. He'd take her by the hand and ask, *Lodi, may I have this one?* And they would move in unison around her kitchen.

The day I told him I wanted to apply to the Peace Corps, Michael disappeared inside himself. It was the first time I'd ever had the feeling of being with someone who had already left. I still miss Michael, miss the straight-forward and surprising way he would say things. We'd be trimming the saplings, working across from each other, moving down the aisles of the greenhouse and he would say, *Splinters only hurt when you touch them.* Now that is true. Or he'd say, *The sun is a common mid-sized yellow star*, and this would put everything in perspective pretty quick.

When I took Michael to meet my mother, he said almost nothing the entire dinner as we sat at the local Thai restaurant staring into our bowls of curry. He answered her questions directly, usually in a phrase. Even though it made for a very awkward meal, there is something about that I admired about his unswerving honesty.

LETTER TO PETER—CLARENCE

Dear Peter,

I have not yet gone on that bus suspended from the roof of City Museum. I thought I would on our last visit, but once I looked at it up close and carefully, I changed my mind.

The paper you write on is great. It is so thick. I have been weighing papers lately, hoping to find the very lightest kind to attach to my balloons. Mom gave me some typing paper that I'm using for the time being until something even thinner comes along. But I love how your paper is so sturdy. It seems like it would last a good long time.

Do you have any idea why someone might own a mannequin? My mom recently got one. It folds at the waist, is a man, his eyes downcast so he looks like he's reading. I do not understand what she needs with it or why she has it. Maybe you will have some thoughts. If so, will you please let me know?

Your pen pal,
Clarence Clark

There. I wrote it. I told him about Mom's foldable man, about Fred. Maybe I'll find out the reason for this oversized doll.

SELF-INVENTION—SARAH

One of my favorite poets is Marina Tsvetaeva, who lost a daughter to starvation during The Moscow Famine. She wrote, *No one has ever stepped into the same river twice.* I love the quotation because it is true both literally — the water's always moving, so it's different — and figuratively true. I wonder if we've lived through enough, we will forget ourselves enough to see such truths. In college, I had a professor who loved Tsvetaeva so much she read her poems aloud to us, one after another, for most of every class. The class was entitled Russian Literature, and so those of us who'd signed up expected reading Dostoyevsky and Pushkin and Gogol. Some of us had heard of Tsvetaeva, but did not think she would be the focus of the course. But I can safely say that others felt as I did. It was utterly delightful. To hear someone read out loud words they love, words which sing in their heart never gets tiresome. It was magical to hear Dr. Landauer's voice lift as she read. When she explained to us the circumstances under which Tsvetaeva wrote a particular poem, we all lifted our heads as if from prayer, then went back to the bent posture.

THE WAY THINGS WORK—CLARENCE

Did you know that 2.7 billion years ago the earth had no trees or animals or flowers or birds or fish, but it did rain? Geologists right here in Missouri figured that one out; found fossilized raindrops to prove it. What this means is the earth was not all ice. I love it when recent discoveries disprove old ones. Just when we think we've got something figured out, boom, it's proven wrong with actual life evidence to back it up.

There are entire books written about things people have come, over time, to understand. Since I was a tiny kid one of my favorites was *The Way Things Work*. Best part is these wooly mammoths who talk amongst themselves about the fact that they will one day be extinct. The book has facts about friction and sound waves and gravity. Gravity: even though we can't see it, it plays a huge role in our lives. It keeps the earth and other planets orbiting around each other. It even affects how much people weigh. Someone who weighs 200 pounds here on earth would only weigh 76 pounds on Mars; no need for that diet, I guess.

Part of me thinks Foldable Fred will always remain in the baffling category; it could be my own unsolvable mystery. And behind that mystery are deeper mysteries still. But things lose luster once you know too much about them. Here's an example: every December Mom gets me an Advent calendar. It contains different shaped chocolates hidden behind miniature doors you open on each of the days leading up to Christmas. Before I open a day's door on the calendar, there is a surprise. Behind door number three might be a bell, or an angel, or a snowflake, or even a reindeer. But as soon as I flip back the cardboard, the suspense is over. It would be an even greater letdown were it not for the joy of the chocolate melting in my mouth.

I think kids love mysteries, but adults not so much. And there are many mysteries. Take five-and-dime stores. My mom says there used to be hordes of them, selling a wide range of inexpensive stuff for your home and your body. They would divide shelves of items into compartments of 5, 10, and 25 cent merchandise. Now they are called Dollar General—but five-and-dime? Why not nickel-and-dime? That mystifies me. And then there are the bigger, more alarming wonders of the world. True story: in 2004 a guy woke up outside a Burger King in Georgia with no clothes, no identification, and no memory. He had absolutely no clue who he was. Take a moment just to imagine not knowing anything about yourself, how old you are, who your mother is, what you have done so far in your life. They even called in the FBI, but no one could figure it out. So, this man, who now goes by the name of Benjamin, lives to this day in a shack in Georgia and washes dishes for a job. Talk about an unsolved mystery.

Sometimes when I'm in line at a store, I imagine that the guy in front of me—the one buying antifreeze or shaving cream—is my dad. And I try to imagine what his life is like by the clothes he is wearing or how he speaks to the cash register person. Then I think about what it would be like to be in the same car, or the same home with this person. I make it in my mind like we both secretly know our relationship but don't want to say anything, so we just go our separate ways. We both figure it will end up being awkward. But what if this happened? What if we found each other? It would be like finding a missing piece to who I am. Imagine.

Maybe I'm lucky, actually. Kids whose parents are divorced are always having to switch back and forth between two homes. They have to lug around a huge backpack with all the stuff they need. They have to ask the school secretary to keep their backpack in the front office because there's no way it will fit in their locker. Plus, what if one parent's house had Wi-Fi and the other one did not, and they needed the internet to do their homework—they'd get stuck in a real predicament. My science partner, David's, parents are divorced and hate each other so much their lawyers forbade them to talk to each other. So, David has to carry this composition book with him so his parents can communicate with written notes about things that happen. If his mom takes him to the dentist, for instance, and the dentist finds a cavity, she has to write it all out in the book. She has to explain it for his father.

I would not like that one bit. At least my mom doesn't have to keep a notebook for someone, and I don't have to grow up in two homes.

And then there's this kid, Miles, whose dad lives in a room over their garage and spends hours at a time walking around Rolla carrying a plastic grocery bag. He wears a blaze orange vest, and even in summer, layer upon layer of coats. His gaze is perpetually cast down at the sidewalk, so he's probably counting his steps, like I used to do. If I ever see him downtown, I just cross to the other side of the street and give him the space he needs for his counting. Miles said he's never heard his dad say one word, but that they sometimes sit together, eat SpaghettiOs, and watch reruns of this show called Bullwinkle, about a bull who talks. So, my dad, like Mom's collapsible man, might just have to live in the mystery category-at least for the time being.

UNDERSTUDY IN MY LIFE—SARAH

After our trip to Maine, Clarence would routinely reenact the stewardess pointing to the exit windows, pulling down oxygen masks, putting on the life vest and explaining how to make it inflate. And he did it pretty much daily. So I asked Sally, the receptionist from First Baptist, to bring me one of her husband's oxygen masks. He's a paramedic, and I knew he'd be more than happy to give Clarence something to fiddle around with. Well, he played with that, kind of made a skit out of it, over and over. What amazed me was his recollection of what the stewardess had said. He could rattle off her speech pretty much verbatim.

It's Friday night, and I've made plans to have dinner with my friend Peggy. I've even hired a sitter, Elizabeth, a college student who volunteers at the "Y" as part of her sociology class. The forecasted late winter snow shows little promise of materializing, even though I had it in my mind that it would quiet the street as I walked home. It's less than a half mile to Rolla's main street where the town's two restaurants reside. I'm thinking of what Elizabeth and Clarence might be doing. I'm thinking about all the things I've given up. I miss teaching, the way the students can lift you out of your own thoughts. I miss having a lover, a man's body to hold. I miss the smell of tomatoes, that spice-filled smell. I miss not worrying about money. I feel like an understudy in my own life, like I'm here studying a role I have to play for someone else.

FAILED EXPERIMENTS—CLARENCE

Today I bought my box of cereal from the discount bin, and the expiration date had long since passed, in January 2018. The marshmallows in the Lucky Charms were like cardboard, bland and crunchy. They were not magically delicious in any way, shape, or form. Like all failed experiments, you learn something through mistakes like these. From the discount bin, I can keep on buying gummy bears because of their super-duper individual foil wrapper, but no more cereal, at least not ones with soft bits.

We're studying cells in science class. First, we had to draw a plant cell and after that, an animal cell. Plant cells are tricky to get just right; there's more stuff in them. Doesn't that seem opposite of what you'd think? Wouldn't you think animal cells would be the more complex of the two? Plus, plant cells are not circular. Circular is easier to draw. At first, I thought it was strange that everything alive has cells. But when you take time to think about it, that makes sense. What else would keep a being alive? Cell growth is what makes babies grow into adults. And we all know that needs to happen.

I'm saving up to get a dog. I am careful to keep this news from Peaches because you know about cats and dogs. That's probably all I need to say. I've compiled a list of reasons we need a dog, and the benefits far outweigh the concerns. Number one: protection. A nice, loud bark once in a while would provide safety. Number two: companionship. While Peaches is soft and warm, her principal activity is sleeping, not hanging out with me. If I try to get her to do something — run after a balled-up piece of paper, for instance — she just yawns and lays her head back down and starts snoring. Number three: exercise. I'd take our dog to the park and let him run until his legs gave out. I see people there throwing sticks and balls for dogs who look so pleased when they bring the object back to their owner repeatedly. It's like a fresh thing every single time.

Most Sundays there is this guy at the park with a metal detector, sweeping it close to the ground. He wears headphones and must occasionally hear a beep because he stops and digs. Me? So far, I've found a twenty-dollar bill (score), an earring in the shape of an acorn, three mittens, a baseball cap and — this is probably the strangest — a postcard from Florida of a couple sunbathing with the caption: *we're sunning so nice, you're shoveling the ice.* That sure seems like a mean thing to send a friend or relative in the mail, given how cold and long our Missouri winters are. It's March, well after St. Patrick's Day, and I'm still wearing my coat and hat and gloves. We are definitely still shoveling the ice.

Yesterday in Mrs. Baker's kindergarten class where I visit my reading buddy once a week, the kids were drawing pictures, free form, anything they wanted. Mrs. Baker stopped in front of this girl — Katie — who was intently working on her picture, bent all the way over it, pressing down on her crayon like there was no tomorrow. When Mrs. Baker asked, *What are you drawing?* Katie established, *I'm drawing God.* Mrs. Baker: *But no one knows what God looks like.* Katie: *Well, they will in a minute.* You have got to admire the way Katie was so self-assured. Little kids have a sureness to them that gets stripped away over time. Kindergarteners are like fresh, new balloons, filled with helium, ready to float up, up, up. They don't yet know that the helium eventually leaks out, loses its buoyancy (this week's word).

Speaking of balloons, since my last report, I've launched nine more and gotten back three postcards. The first was from St. James — the next town over. The second came from a student at Missouri University of Science and Technology right here in Rolla. He is an engineer and said my idea was inventive — which felt good coming from someone who is going to school to learn to be an inventor, to be an engineer. The third response was from Plato, Missouri, which is almost as far away as St. Louis, but in the other direction. It must have gotten caught in some storm because all the other balloons have been pulled east. That post card contained lots of information, quite official. It read: *Your balloon has landed in the mean center of the United States. If you spread a flat map of the*

United States, it would balance perfectly if a weight of identical value represented every living person.

It took me awhile to understand what this meant, but now I get it: if a one pound weight stood in for every living person then the map would balance perfectly in Plato, 80 miles from Rolla. There would be the same number of people to the west as to the east, to the north as to the south, to the southwest as to the northeast. This got me to thinking: what if everyone stood on one side of the world? Would it flip over? Or if everyone jumped up in the air at the same time—what would happen then? What about all those people leaving the north each fall to live in Florida for the winter? Does that affect the spinning of the earth? Mom came with me the week I set the St. James balloon free. We stood side by side watching it float far out of sight.

NEVER ENOUGH—SARAH

All the articles about parenting that I tell myself not to read—but end up ensconced in—state with evidence that children raised by a single parent have a much tougher go of it in life. They have a harder time in school and a harder time with peers. The research argues that these children have not had the example of two people negotiating at home, so they will be ill equipped to negotiate out in the world. The Eskimos had an outstanding idea. Why not huddle up together and share the tasks? They shared the burdens and the triumphs and survived well that way. Sometimes I think, albeit briefly, of what it would be like to be in an old style polygamous Mormon relationship. Maybe that way Clarence could have many moms to look after him. He'd have choices of whom to ask depending on his question. I think about these things most while cleaning the church kitchen, swirling the mop in the warm bucket of Spic and Span. Sometimes I realize I've been standing over that bucket for a full minute watching the bubbles make new formations, sometimes in the shape of animals, other times hearts.

I brought the mannequin home from Henry's vacant office so it would look like someone is in the apartment, so it would look like someone is awake at night. I'll admit it is strange to live in what used to be a store, but the rent won't change. It won't go up every year. They promised me that. So, I have that peace of mind. Before we moved in, before Clarence could even sit up, I had dividers brought in so the apartment would have rooms—or at least quasi rooms. Now the kitchen has a wall separating it from the living room. Clarence and I each have a room of our own. It was less expensive to have the dividers be the kind offices use which are just cubicles and don't go all the way to the ceiling. But it works and is better than having our home be one gigantic room.

At night, though, since the front window is over forty feet wide, a person passing by can see into the living room even through the curtains. You'd have to put up a blackout curtain to achieve complete privacy, and I didn't want to go that far. So, I came up with the idea of setting up the mannequin in a slightly different position each night before I leave for work. That way it appears as if a man is sitting reading the newspaper. If someone drives by and looks in the apartment, it will seem like someone is home and awake, faithfully guarding the place. At least this is how I bought myself peace of mind enough to leave for work.

The Greeks believed those who were blind to the physical world had special insight. Tiresias even put out his own eyes to better see what was hidden. Clarence has amazing insight, inward seeing. I think that is part of what makes it so hard for him to get through a day. It's like he sees more than the rest of us, sees things we miss. And I don't want to have to add to his burden ever.

UNIVERSAL LOST AND FOUND—CLARENCE

You know how most schools, movie theaters—even the Y—have lost and founds, a box or closet where they put stuff people have left behind. It's usually pretty crammed with stuff, and musty smelling, but it contains magic. It's the place for keeping possessions people have lost and can someday reclaim. What a brilliant thing! But where do you bring the stray mitten you find on 11th street, the one that looks to be handmade by someone's grandma? Or the flip-flop floating in a river? Or the hubcap flung onto a soccer field? We've all seen people prop that hubcap by the side of the road. But how often do you think the rightful owner really drives there and says, *oh, that's my hubcap, how great!* The times I've lost something—last week it was my field trip permission form—I have felt like part of me was lost. There was this gnawing sensation that something was utterly and deeply wrong. In fifth grade I left the watch my uncle had given me for my ninth birthday at the pool. I remembered taking it off and putting it in my pocket before I went into the water. But when I got in Mom's car after the pool was closed, no watch. I will never know what happened to the watch. I never found the watch. It still feels off kilter, like a picture hanging crooked on a wall. Like wondering who my dad is.

So, what if there were a universal lost and found where all the things people have ever misplaced or left or dropped were stored? That would be pretty great. The summer Mom and I went to Maine, after our flight back home, our luggage did not come tumbling out on the conveyor belt with all the other black roller bags. We recognized two people from our flight, including the guy who sat in the aisle seat next to Mom and snored the entire time. After all our fellow travelers got their bags and merrily wheeled them out of the terminal, the conveyor belt kept on going. But it remained empty, nothing on it, *click clack, click clack, click clack*, very empty. We ended up in the lost baggage office. It is this one room with a guy, and behind him another room filled top to bottom with what must be unclaimed luggage. What if there were a place like that which held all things people had ever, ever lost? It would be a universal lost and found.

Mom says there is a lost and found for mail. It's called a dead letter office, an entire office dedicated to letters stamped "return to sender" or "no such address" or "no address on file". I wonder if my dad would go to the lost and found places looking for me if there were such places. But maybe my dad is just dead, plain and simple. Maybe Mom doesn't want to tell me he died in a terrible fire. Or that he was shot at a hold-up in the 7-11; shot at gunpoint right through the heart. Maybe she doesn't want me envisioning that over and over for the rest of my life. But if he's dead, then there would be a gravestone somewhere that I could visit. I would bring rocks and pile them on his stone. I would tell myself that the piled rocks were keeping him warm.

LESSONS I'D LIKE TO UNLEARN—SARAH

My mother taught me to distrust most people. She'd take off her glasses, fog them with her breath, wipe them on the corner of her sleeve and list reasons to keep your wits about you, reasons never to let down your guard; to be on the lookout at all times. I must have been only ten when I took to calling her Margaret instead of Mom. Unconsciously I was putting a distance between us, stripping her of the role of mother in my life. How terrified of the world Margaret must have been. She wanted to impart in me a healthy dose of that fear. She would routinely say, "you can't trust a stranger". "You can't trust a boss". "You can't even trust a friend, so why have one?" Most of her life lessons are ones I'd like to unlearn. But that's harder to do than you'd think: undoing what's instilled in you from birth. Stark is the word that comes to mind when I try to describe my mother, stark and stiff and unforgiving.

So, when I met Henry, I agreed with myself to let go, to trust and to trust fully, to trust without restraint. I was out to prove my mother wrong, show her and me both that fear and holding back have no place when it comes to loving relationships. When Clarence started kindergarten, I'd wait at the end of the school day in the chair next to the door until the school bus brakes puffed out their air. Then I'd scurry out to the bus stop. The way my heart felt seeing him trundle down the stairs with a paper or two clutched in one hand, backpack in the other was like a faucet pouring out, suddenly freed of its hold. So even though Henry proved me wrong, my love is boundless. Of that I can be sure. And so, Margaret's dementia is a relief because she cannot be as judgmental and critical. She lives in her memories, and how she sees what happened in her life has softened substantially in recent years.

KING TUT HAD A MANNEQUIN TOO—CLARENCE

One thing I really hate is giving people directions. A few weeks ago, Mom's college roommate came to visit. Mom had gone to Kroger and left her phone on the kitchen table. The third time it rang from the same number, I picked it up, and it was Mary, Mom's friend. She said she was on Canal Street and needed to know which way to go. I found myself suddenly and completely at a loss for words. What I got out was, *What are you looking at?* If you think about it, that's a personal question to ask someone you've never met. When I eventually figured out in my mind where Mary was, and where she needed to take a left and where to take a right, a lot of time had definitely passed. This is why I'm not much for giving directions. I'm pretty sure the other person becomes exasperated with the delay in answering, while I wait for what to say.

Once when I was walking home from returning a DVD at Family Video, a store I'll tell you about later, a guy stopped me and asked how to get to the CVS. Now, that store is literally three blocks from where I was, but I looked at him as if he had two heads and told a complete lie. I told him I was not from Rolla, that I was just visiting. If I had a do-over on that one, I'd just offer to walk the guy there. I'd be like one of those tour guides who are pointing out the obvious things. I'd say, *Over there is the college bookstore where students get what they need for class. And next to it is Pace Jewelers, where there are some fancy rings locked up under glass.*

When I was in second grade, Mom had her high school teaching job, which meant I had to stay for the after-school program. As soon as the after-school teachers let us out of the cafeteria—where we were perpetually gluing cotton balls onto blue paper to make snowmen—I'd run as fast as my legs would take me to the swings and try to get the swing to loop over the top of the set. I'd pump and pump my legs with such force you'd think I was trying to kick off my shoes. I felt 100% sure that if I got high enough, I'd soar over the top of that set. The teacher,

Miss Polly, said, *Trust me, Clarence, it is physically impossible for the swing to loop over the set.* Well, she couldn't have chosen better words to motivate me. Whenever someone says *trust me*, I get suspicious. *Trust me, that won't work, Trust me, it's not time. Trust me, it will rain tomorrow. Trust me, this shot won't hurt.* Those very words show the possibility of mistrust. Why else even say them?

I figured out how to temporarily get my mind off something bad, or sad, or scary. I focus on measurements, the actual size of objects close by. How many feet wide is the floor of the room? How high is the ceiling? How tall is the bookcase? Did you know barleycorn was for a long time the principle unit of measurement? A barleycorn is exactly one-third of an inch. And today's shoe sizes come directly from this. A size eight shoe is one barleycorn larger than a size seven. Now that's something to not forget.

Somewhat related to this is how people say, "He's got 80 head of cattle?" If the dude had only cow heads, that sure would be spooky. But that's the way farmers — believe me I know because it can get rural real fast here in Rolla — talk about what they raise or what ranges their land. Secretly I find these phrases wondrous. And I like the way someone will say *I bought a painting for a song.* For a song! Maybe once upon a time people could pay by entertaining, by singing a song in exchange for something. I must look that up. Now that I think about it, people still do. Think Hollywood. Think Nashville. And those guys get paid a lot to sing and act.

Try as I might I can't stop wondering about Fred; can't get my mind off that mannequin. But here's the catch: ever since his arrival, Mom has seemed happier, more peaceful. It's like someone has taken a scrub brush and erased a few of her worries. Now she seems more easy going. After school on Tuesday, while I was eating my Smart Start, and she was drinking coffee at the kitchen table, I challenged her to a staring contest — something we occasionally do. Before we began, she smiled and said, *You know whooooo would win?* An owl would win. And she was right. Do owls ever blink? At least in photos they always look terrifically wide awake. It's strange that they sleep when we're awake, and we sleep when they're awake. We are opposites. Maybe that's why many people are so drawn to them. We are curious about their night lives.

They must be curious about our day lives. I like screech owls the most. Not only because of their name — screech — but also because they are cute, puffy little guys you want to hold in the palm of your hand.

More proof of Mom's newfound peace of mind is that she's started sitting down and doing things with me more often. Last weekend we watched a movie on video about a kid whose family went on a trip over Christmas and left him behind, home alone, by mistake. That is the title of the movie, Home Alone. Anyway, while the kid's parents were frantically trying to get back to him, the kid was having the time of his life. That is until he found out that some robbers were planning on breaking into his house because they thought everyone was gone. So that night the kid turned on all the lights, played music on his speakers real loud, and propped clothes he'd stuffed with other clothes in front of the windows to make it look like someone was in the house. The kid made quasi-mannequins like you do a scarecrow. When I saw them, I looked over at Mom because I wanted to see if she'd react when she saw those mannequins. But she didn't.

I'm sure hoping Peter will have some thoughts about Fred, the collapsible man. I figure I was definitely safe telling him since there's no chance he'll come visit, given his allergy to cats and his suspicion of cars. In my next letter, I will mention Peaches a lot, slip in some tidbits about her, maybe even include a photo. That will keep him from venturing to visit to us.

Peter wrote back, took him two weeks this time. And guess what? He sent me a photo! We must be on the same wavelength.

Dear Clarence,

It's been cold and windy here in St. Louis. I hope you are keeping as warm as possible. Sometimes I wear two coats. Do you ever do that?

As far as the mannequin goes, I know that people have long held a fascination with them. When archeologists opened King Tut's tomb in 1923, they discovered an armless, legless, wooden torso, the same size as the pharaoh. So, people's interest in mannequins goes back at least to ancient Egypt. In the 13th century, Marie Antoinette, the queen of France, sent small sized mannequins to her mother and sister so they could get a taste of the latest fashions at the Palace of Versailles. So, it seems possible that your mom is someone else with an interest in mannequins. If I were you, I wouldn't worry. I bet there is an excellent reason she has one, which you will find out when the time is just right.

Here is another, more personal mannequin connection. One of the first jobs I ever had was at the Nevada Nuclear Test Site. It was 1955, the year they were doing lots of above ground nuclear bomb explosions to understand the effects, and my job was to arrange mannequins in life-sized doll houses within the blast zone where the atomic bombs were being detonated. I then had to do inspections to see what the blast did to the mannequins. I can tell you I am sure glad that is not a job I kept for very long. It was truly ghastly.

Well, I'll get this in the mail to you. I include a picture of Linus I took last summer. He is sitting soaking up the sun at the park where I take him for walks on pleasant days.

Your pen pal,
Peter

His dog Linus is jet black with a huge, blocky head. Well, Peter is right about Mom liking history. She is all the time reading biographies of famous people: Winston Churchill, Marie Curie, George Washington Carver, Nelson Mandela. I'm amazed about King Tut and his mannequin. In fifth grade, we learned some cool stuff about him, how he was just a kid when he ruled Egypt. He got the job when he was nine years old. But no one ever told us about the mannequin King Tut had. So now, I have a little more information, a fact I can bring up and maybe get Mom to talk about Fred and her reasons for having him.

WHO DID WHAT AND WHEN—SARAH

The peculiar thing about reading a magnificent book is you embrace a ready-made conflict. You want to read the book, do nothing in the world but just read it, but you also don't want it ever to end. If I love a book, I read it slowly, savoring it. The problem with that is I lose track of the plot. I'm focusing more on the sentences, on how each individual word is used, so I forget who did what and when. Maybe that is not so bad. Maybe we can read for plot and also read just to read. At least that seems to be the case with me. My one rule for a book is that it must make you question your own life. It needs to shake things up and review, examine, alter your life. Even if a book only makes you reexamine your habit of washing dishes by hand, that is enough for it to be a wonderful book.

Books slow things down. Time, which seems only to race out of control, becomes simpler and slower when reading. That's another requirement I have for a book: it needs to slow things down. Movies do not accomplish this. They skip vast parcels of time to move the plot along; but books, they let you rest awhile, mull things over. That may be the very best part. That and how you get a do-over. You can read a book twice, three times, eighteen times, and always pick up on something new and unexpected with each read.

A book speaks directly to you. Not like a person speaking with you who might check a cellphone text or distractedly pick their cuticles. A book is the speaker telling you what they want to tell you, without distraction. Sometimes it's like the lift your stomach gets on a steep and windy country road, when cresting a hill, it may lurch up into your throat. That's how powerfully and physically a glorious book can move you.

Nobody at the Y reads much, except Reader's Digest magazines, which is an unfortunate publication. Why make a shortened, watered-down version of something? That seems a travesty. So, among the people I'm around, I'm pretty much alone in my reading life, just me and my books. That's how much of the rest of my life is, except for time spent with Clarence.

DISTORTION—CLARENCE

Mom says it is good that I was born in the time in history when I was; that even if I'd lived fifteen years earlier, people would not have understood my Asperger's influenced behavior in the way they do now. She said I would have had more people saying mean things to me. She said people used to be more critical of disabilities, to magnify them. Sometimes we play a game we call "Count Your Lucky Stars." It involves listing the things we're thankful for. And Mom always says that she's super grateful I was born. But also thankful I was born in these more enlightened times regarding the spectrum of autism. Today I'm thankful for trees. They seem so happy just being what they are. Mostly they stand tall, proud, strong, and contented. When I told Mom that, she quoted a writer she loves: *I like trees because they seem more resigned to the way they have to live than other things do.*[3]

Distortion, in geography, means that if you take the earth and make it flat on a map, reality changes based on how you do it. What happens with the more common world maps is that certain parts get enlarged, making the countries in the northern part of the world appear much bigger than they are in relation to the countries in the south. Greenland, for instance, appears bigger than Australia when in reality it is smaller. Last Christmas Mom gave me a pair of heavy, black binoculars. She said she'd found them at Vintage Thrift. What I like best is how you can look through them both ways. If I look through the narrower end, objects appear closer, so close, actually, that it makes me feel dizzy. If I look in the larger end, things seem far away. The cut cornfield beside the highway looks, through the large end of my binoculars, like the ground needs to get a shave, like it's sporting a five o'clock shadow. But through

---

[3] Willa Cather

the small end the cows are gigantic, way oversized. You can even see the indentations in their wet black noses.

Kevin, the bus driver I've had since first grade, always had a pair of binoculars hanging from the back of his seat. I suppose he used them to birdwatch when he had a spare moment or two, perhaps when in the school driveway waiting for classes to let out. But Kevin was just outright gone one day. On Tuesday, he was driving us like normal and on Wednesday, no Kevin. There must have been some kind of actual emergency in his life because the guy seemed to live for his job. And it was not only Halloween that proved this. Every Friday he would dress up with white gloves and a chauffeur's cap. At the end of each month he would hand out homemade chocolate chip cookies, individually wrapped. At any stop where there were little kids waiting with their parents, he'd pull up extra slow, then talk to each child who lumbered up the stairs. He would say things like, *Miles, I like your shirt today*, and *Kylie, that is one magnificent pair of shoes*. Talk about making a difference in people's lives in small ways. He made the bus ride into a mini party every single day. And he still misses the 80s. Sometimes he would even bring his radio and tune the station to the oldies. When a song came on that he liked, he'd tap both his index fingers on the steering wheel in time with the music. You could just tell he was happy, that his job was the exact thing he wanted to be doing.

But last week, in Kevin's place, there was this spectacularly grumpy looking lady with white hair pulled tight into a bun; not the person you want to ask anything of. All I could think of, when I saw her, was how much her head must hurt with her hair under tension like that. That morning five kids at my stop—I make the sixth—dutifully and silently climbed on and took our seats, no one asking where Kevin might be. I usually sit right in the middle of the bus—the hump seat we call it; the one where the wheel well comes through. I sit with Calvin, who can produce these clicking noises with his tongue that make you believe there's an oversized beetle in the nearby vicinity. By minute three of our ride with bun lady, Calvin gnarled his face up and looked at me. That made me laugh on the inside so hard I could not contain it, so I stood up because it was all just too much. That is when bun lady got on the intercom and barked out, *Sit down and calm down, everyone just sit down and calm down. Boy in the middle of the bus, that means you. Sit down. Calm down.*

Truth be told, it had never even occurred to me that school buses came equipped with intercoms. On field trips when we ride a charter bus, our teacher uses the Americabus Company's intercom to give us the lay of the land for what to do when we get to our destination: what the rules are and where we will meet for lunch. But Kevin had not once used the intercom on the school bus. Not once in my six years of riding his bus. And by the end of that first ride with Ms. Bun we'd heard "sit down and calm down" nine times. Calvin and I started putting marks — like this: IIII — in his English composition book every time she said it. Day one, intercom usage: 14. Day two totaled in at 16. Now brace yourself: yesterday the intercom broke. Yes, it did. You should have seen the look on Bun's face as she was talking into it, but it didn't broadcast what she was trying to get across to us. She was talking — you could see her lips in the gigantic rearview mirror — and her face was getting redder and redder and redder, but there was no sound to be heard. Part of me felt sorry for her, but another part thought maybe it was a lesson she needed to learn if she would hang out with middle schoolers for a living. Now I'm missing Kevin; I'm waiting each day for him to get back. Hopefully he'll have a great reason why he was gone. Maybe he got a puppy he needed to stay home with until it was house-trained. I will make it in my mind that's why he's been out. I will look forward to seeing a picture of the puppy when he gets back.

WINTER LANDSCAPE PORTRAIT—SARAH

The hills here in south central Missouri are blunt and chrome, full of intolerable wind. In bitter winter there is always a thin crust of crunch underfoot; not much beauty or comfort in these months of the year. And so, we all rejoice come St. Patrick's Day when the air softens long enough to let you hope that spring will come at last. Even the sculpture of the trees has a blandness, the heavy winds pulling at them without relent, maddeningly. And so I read. My current novel, translated from Italian, is entitled "The Days of Abandonment". Like most of the books I love, it's hard to say what it's about. There's the regret of motherhood, loneliness, suspicion and anxiety and disfigurement. And there's this sentence: *we carry in our head until we die the living and the dead*. I like the word carry there. Because the word comes from the Latin for a wheeled vehicle, there is a sense of rolling along, of ease. We carry them — maybe that carriage is easy.

HEROIC ACTS—CLARENCE

Whenever I ask Mom about her parents, I get the sense there is something she wants to say but won't or can't. Her dad died of a heart attack. I was able to find that out. And I think about that moment for Mom: just like that and no more dad. He was at work, so Mom got the news over the phone. The one time I pried her about it, and kept on asking questions about him, her face tightened in a way that told me not to ask anymore. After a lengthy silence, she looked at me and established, *He was an intellectual and a loner.* Bang, and a door shut between us; I knew I'd asked too much. Or in a way that forced her to put a label on what she herself did not, or could not, or would never understand. Loner is a final and drastic thing to say about someone.

But Mom will talk about her grandfather, her dad's dad, all you want. He was a farmer, raised cattle, and had a garden that fed the entire family for six months out of the year. His name was Chalmers and his sister — what would be my great grandaunt — was Alice. Mom explained the significance of their names: Allis-Chalmers is a tractor company, like John Deere. So, they named their kids after a tractor. Pretty cool. But I never met him, my great grandfather. Mom says he walked around whistling; all the time whistling melodies to church hymns, to *Onward Christian Soldiers* or *Bringing in The Sheaves*. He couldn't sneak up on anybody. There was a constant soundtrack floating in the air surrounding him.

Mom has a home movie — she'd converted it to a DVD from a VHS — featuring the day her grandfather taught her how to ride a bike. The film is silent, but you can tell exactly what is happening. It begins with initial instructions, with Chalmers holding onto the back of the bike seat while Mom is practicing pedaling, braking, and balancing. And then Mom is launched. She is off on her own — with wind in her face. She is independently heading out into the world. I'm wondering now who took the movie, standing down the road a bit to capture the action. Was it Alice? Was it a neighbor? Was it her own mother? I have the feeling I will never know.

Mom is all the time giving me glimpses of this lady who took care of her when she was young, starting from when she was six weeks old. Anna lived in a teeny tiny bright yellow house. She wore calico dresses, men's shoes, and had two long grey braids. She had once worked the night shift at a frozen food factory, putting turkey into the TV dinners. She stood by a conveyor belt eight hours a day, scooping chunks of white meat into aluminum trays. She did this for thirty years until the day she noticed a foul smell to some meat. She immediately pulled the cord above her head to call her supervisor. When he arrived at her station, he loomed over Anna and told her to keep on going, keep on packing the meat into the trays. He said it wasn't her place to say anything. Her job was to pack the meat, and that was all. Well, Anna would not make people sick, so she stepped back from the conveyor belt, took off the rubber apron she'd been wearing and quit, right then and there. Mom said that is one fine example of heroism. She stuck to her guns, did what she knew in her heart was right, even though it cost her her job.

Until last year, Mom's mom lived at Parkside Assisted Care in St. Louis. We'd go visit her every couple of months. I called her Meemaw, but Mom always called her Margaret, which strikes me as strange. It seems to me if a person is your mom you would say "mom". But that's a story for another time. Usually when we visited, Meemaw was hanging out in her room, watching TV on mute or staring at her fingers as if they held an answer to a question she'd been mulling over for days. She had dementia, which made her forget things that were happening in the here and now. But she could remember her childhood. She could remember stunning details about what it was like when she was ten. She walked to school every day and with her best friend would pick little yellow flowers called buttercups. They would hold the flower under each other's chin, and if the buttercup cast a deep yellow color, that meant that person liked butter. She remembered things from when she was young a lot better than any other adult I know. For that reason, she was easy to relate to.

One time she described playing jump rope, the kind with a long rope with two people swinging it. She thought it taught an important life lesson, because once the rope is in motion you have to just jump into it. There is no time to sit back and decide if it's a good idea or not. She said most things in life are like that: you just need to jump in. *Put your fears in your back pocket*, is what she said, *and go*. She pronounced the word go quickly, like she would do the jumping. She said there's no way to fall, only to get tangled up in the rope. She said the only falling happens if you don't try. She could even drum up the names of the girls holding the two ends of the rope: Beth and Claire. And she could sing all the words to the songs they used to sing as they swung the rope: *Miss Mary Mac Mac Mac, all dressed in black, black, black with silver buttons, buttons, buttons all down her back, back, back.* I liked her stories and songs a lot, kind of like being at a movie. But I could tell Mom just wanted the visit to be over. All I can figure is Mom just wanted her old mom back, the one who could remember what day of the week it was and whether she had eaten lunch.

The last time we visited, Meemaw was in the nursing home common room, which is a big linoleum floored place with puffy plastic chairs. And the room was packed, everyone staring at the TV watching golf. Apparently, it was the Masters, an enormous deal in golf. And Meemaw was visibly enthralled. So, we stood near the back of the room watching her and the other people who lived in the nursing home watch this slow-moving game on a big green field. I thought how it was like watching an aquarium, the fluid, arching movements of the players and the ball that looks to be floating. As soon as she saw us Meemaw looked at me in this otherworldly way and asked, *Does your father still play golf?* And it felt like there was a crash of thunder in my ears. Before I could say anything, Mom barked, *We don't talk about Clarence's father. I have told you that more times than I can count. Please, Margaret, try to remember something I say.* So Meemaw just turned and started staring at the TV again, following the colors and movements on the golf course.

THE TININESS OF CLEMENTINES—SARAH

After Clarence could eat any food as a baby, after we'd done the week with rice cereal, week with green beans, week with applesauce, and ruled out all allergies the way the pediatrician advised, I unearthed his love for clementines. The first time he held the little clementine segment between his thumb and index finger and marveled at the wonder of it, I suspected that this was the fruit for him. A few years later he held a clementine segment in the same way and proclaimed, *Look, it's already cut for you.* After that, I took to calling him Clementine Clarence for a few weeks, and he smiled whenever I said it.

THINGS THAT HAPPEN IN THE SAME DAY— CLARENCE

Today, in the mail, there's a letter from Peter, but it is addressed to Sarah and Clarence Clark, not just to me. Mom's at the Y until 8:00 pm, so I have a long time to wait to solve this mystery. I knew she'd written down Peter's address, and I guessed that she might try to get in touch with him, check out who my pen pal was. But now he's written us back, and I'm more than curious to know what he's said. I will head over to Rent-to-Own, watch TV, and pass some time with Larry.

The news is showing on the wide-screen above my regular sitting spot, and since Larry is busy with a customer. I might as well just make myself at home with a big bag of popcorn in my La-Z-Boy. Here are some of today's news stories: in Brazil a 3D printer made a beak for a toucan the police had rescued. The bird was missing her top beak. Veterinarians figured she'd lost it in a fight with another toucan. And today a retired post office worker found a message in a bottle that was over a hundred years old. A retired post office worker — someone whose job had been to deliver letters, which are, after all, just messages — found one on a beach while vacationing. Next there's a story about a plane in Siberia that got stuck on the runway, so the passengers got out and pushed. It looked so cold, all these people bundled in coats and gloves and fur hats, the likes of which I've never seen, even here at the edge of the Ozarks where winter's wind whips across the plains. The last story took place in Iowa. It was about a barber giving free haircuts to children in exchange for them reading stories to him. You have to be younger than 13, but that sure is one impressive way to get kids to read. And all these things happened today. Plus, that letter from Peter sits on the kitchen table waiting to be opened.

After my time at Rent-to-Own, I head on back to the apartment thinking I might take this opportunity to check out foldable Fred again.

Mom keeps him in his case under her bed. Before that, I end up fiddling with a doll Mom saved from when she was young. It's about a foot tall and made of plastic, with blond, stiff hair. Instead of a belly button, there's a knob in her stomach and when you turn it, the doll's hair gets longer and longer and longer, it plays out from the center of the doll's head, making this oversized ponytail. At Walmart, I've seen dolls that can eat and pee and even cry. Now, why in the world would you want that? I guess this mannequin is nothing more than an oversized doll made to look like a grownup. If I think of it that way, it's not so weird. Plus, it doesn't pee or cry. When I put the doll back, I spot something I have never noticed before. It's a bright colored Hawaiian looking man's shirts in the back of Mom's closet. I take it out slowly, hold it and smell it. It's musty.

And then an idea hits me. Mom's mannequin needs a little color. He will look much more cheerful in the Hawaiian shirt. I open Fred's case. There he lies, so still and alone. I begin by unbuttoning his suit jacket. There are three buttons, so the jacket is easy to get off. After that, I make Fred sit up, which feels creepy. I prop him up in his case and for a moment it's like a corpse has sat up in its coffin, but I try to get that out of my mind by taking off the white button-down shirt he's wearing. It has short sleeves so is easier to remove than I'd expected. Finally, I maneuver — another collected word — his left arm and then his right arm through the armholes in the Hawaiian shirt. This is definitely the trickiest part because his body is made of a hard plastic. But I manage, finally. And I am satisfied. Now Mom's man looks much more cheerful. He looks ready to go to a cookout or maybe even to go bowling. It is all much better now. Everything is better. After some time of beholding this new Fred, I am careful to fold his banker's getup neatly and tuck it into the case beside him. Then I close up the case and put the newly attired mannequin back under Mom's bed. When she opens it again — not sure when that will be — she will be shocked to see him dressed this way. She will want to talk with me about why I did this, and it may be a way for me to get more information as to why she has him.

After I leave Mom's room, I turn on the radio and the same song is playing on two stations even though the stations are not exactly at the same place in the song. If I flip between the two, I get to hear the words a second time. On one station it's, *And anytime you feel the pain, hey Jude refrain*. And on the next station: *The minute you let her under your skin, then you begin to make it better*. When I turn back to the first station I hear, *The minute you let her under your skin, you make it better*, a second time. It's like hearing an echo. This has happened to me only twice in my life, and today is one of those times. I feel like I'm getting to live the same moment twice. I'm getting an automatic do-over without even trying.

Sometimes when Mom listens to the news on the radio, she talks back to it, agrees with it, or has a kind of mini argument with it. She'll say, *That is definitely true* or *Well, what are we going to do about that?* I'll be in my room, while she's in the kitchen with the radio on, and I can hear her having a conversation with the radio. It's like she has a friend in a box on top of the refrigerator, a friend who'll never leave her. She even makes plans with it: *Let's go to that movie*, she'll say to the radio, *We definitely need to check that one out*.

COMEDY RESTORES ORDER—SARAH

There is a guy who answers phones at a local help center for a computer company, you know the kind where you call in and ask questions; the kind where you have to wait incessantly to talk to an actual human being. Well, this guy—let's call him Bob—made a list of the most outrageous calls he has ever received. Here is one: a woman says, *I want to order a new coffee mug holder for my computer.* Bob calmly replies, *I don't think our computers come with coffee mug holders.* Call-in Lady: *Oh, yea they do, this little thing that pops out and you can put your coffee mug in it.* She, of course, meant the disk drive. And the hilarious part was how calm Bob remained throughout the call. He remained steady and kind as he explained to the woman her error. I laughed out loud when I heard this story on the radio this afternoon. Both Clarence and I were laughing in the car uproariously. It was on our way back from the "Y" where he'd sat reading while I did my Saturday shift, and he had been strangely silent the whole ride, like there was something he wanted to ask, but wouldn't or couldn't. And Bob's story cleared the air between, just like that. Aristotle was right. Comedy restores order.

When I was younger, I thought all I had to do for things to be better was to wish. I thought maybe if I wished hard enough my father would pop back to life, and I could get to know him once and for all. He'd come back and take off the mask he wore, I suppose, to protect himself from feeling too much. I often think how much harder things are for Clarence. At least I knew my father. At least I had him in my life for nine years. But I still can't bring myself to tell Clarence about his father, at least not yet. At times, I say to myself, *you're keeping part of him from him, a part he deserves to know, has the right to know.* And this makes me hate myself more often than I'd like to say. Self-loathing is definitely the right word for it. Loathe is a low, deep word, like something under the ocean. It makes you almost groan when you say it. It's apt, though. It fits.

LETTER TO BOTH OF US—CLARENCE

I hear the door clicking, which means Mom is home. I will act all casual, like I am not literally dying for her to open the letter from Peter. When she walks into the kitchen, she sees it straight away, says, *Oh, Peter wrote to the both of us. Let's have a sit down and read it.* She pours herself a cup of sweet tea and opens the letter with a butter knife.

Dear Sarah and Clarence,

I thought I'd take this chance to write the two of you together in one letter. Thank you, Sarah, for your note. To assuage any fears regarding your son's new pen pal, I thought I'd tell you some things about me. I teach two sections of creative writing at St. Louis Community College. While I don't have children of my own, I have two nephews who spend a weekend each month with me. One of them is twelve. When I found Clarence's balloon with the note tied to it, I thought he must be an engineering student at Missouri University of Science and Technology conducting a study of the wind. It was quite a delightful surprise to find out he is so young and so very resourceful. He writes impressively well too.

I am enchanted to have a pen pal in Clarence. My principal occupation, aside from teaching, is writing poetry. I have a few collections that I'd be happy to send to you if you would like.

I shall await your reply.

My very best,
Peter

I could tell, straight away, that Mom felt more than okay about Peter's writing to me now, like a sense of relief had flown in on the wind through that letter. I asked her what "assuage" meant, and she said "ease". Yet there was something in her voice as she read the part about him being a writing teacher that made me look up just for a moment. She's always saying how she likes the plain-spokenness and genuineness of people around Rolla. You get the sense she's been around people who say things they don't really mean. Maybe someone hurt her real bad that way.

MANNEQUIN REDRESSED—SARAH

When I go to get out the mannequin and arrange it in the window, I can't believe what I see. Instead of his business suit, the mannequin has on the one shirt I saved that belonged to Henry. I thought its brightness and easy-going Hawaiian style would be at least bearable in years to come. But seeing the mannequin dressed in it makes me feel physically sick. I want to rip it into shreds. I want to rip it into the most unrecognizable pieces you can imagine. The cheap buttons pop off easily enough, fly into the air, then scatter on the rug of my bedroom floor. But it's harder than I thought to take off the shirt, to get the mannequin's stiff arms through the armholes. I have to wedge the arms at an angle that looks disjointed. But I finally manage. And I just lie down on the bed, unmoving, like something has hit me.

These twelve years I've held it all together relatively well—for Clarence, for us, for the sake of stability. But this is too much. This is just too much to take. They say it takes one moment for a person to snap. All that I've given up, all that I've sacrificed, comes flooding in front of me like a movie in fast forward. People try to be helpful and kind, to offer their suggestions and support, but it is me and Clarence and the Asperger's. It's like a whole other presence, another full-fledged responsibility.

For what must be twenty minutes I lie on the bed, not even realizing I'm clutching Henry's shirt. But now I do. On the bottom left is a weak spot, and I just begin tearing. It comes apart readily in neat strips. Fifteen of them, I count. It feels good to have the shirt in these shreds, feels like I've accomplished what I needed to.

OTHER SENSES—CLARENCE

For her dog's birthday, our upstairs neighbor took her dog—Charlie is his name—on a walk and let him stop and smell any odor of interest for as long as he wanted. She told me about it afterwards, said it took her 90 minutes to go less than a mile. She said that on any other day they would walk that distance in less than 30 minutes. But she said it was peaceful because there was no rush to get anywhere. She and Charlie would take a few steps, then stop for some sniffing, take a few steps, then another sniffing stop. Plus, she didn't have to yank on Charlie's leash. She said next time she needs to go out of town for work she'll ask me to dog sit. I'll definitely do the unlimited smelling walk with Charlie. It must be fantastic to be a dog and be able to discover all kinds of things about what has happened that you did not see just by smelling the scents that have been left by people, animals, and by other dogs. Maybe when I get my dog we will go on frequent smelling walks, and not just on his birthday.

On my walks around Rolla, I check out what the church signs say. This week, the sign at the church near Bear Park says, *There are some questions Google can't answer.* This got me thinking Google doesn't answer questions. Google is a bank of answers where you can look things up. It's not like Google has the answer. Mom said when she was a kid you had to ask your parents a lot more questions because there was no worldwide web and internet search engine. There were encyclopedias, but she said it took way too long to find out what you needed to know. Plus, the encyclopedias were heavy. And their paper was slick and smelled funny. Last year in history our teacher made us look things up one day using only the printed volumes of *The Encyclopedia Britannica.* And I must agree with Mom that the paper is sort of sketchy, like it's made of a substance you cannot describe.

After seeing that church sign about Google, I Google church signs, and I came upon a few that really knocked my socks off—which, come to think of it, seems like an unrealistic thing to say as an expression. That's why I like to use it. How could something knock a person's socks off? I mean, socks are one of those pieces of clothing that are awkward to get off, like wet swimsuits and snow boots. They don't just come off easily. But back to the memorable church signs. Here are two I thought were clever: *Having trouble sleeping? Come listen to our sermons.* And here's a second one: *How do we make holy water? We boil the hell out of it.*

Whenever I ride an elevator—which is rarely as there are not that many of them here in Rolla—I jump up in the air repeatedly as the elevator descends. That way, I spend an extra split second in the air, like a second of flying. Next to the buttons with floor numbers are the same numbers in braille. You can run your hands over them and imagine what a blind person has to go through to get from one place to the next. So far, I've memorized one through seven in braille. I have it in my mind how the dots work for each one.

In third grade, there was a blind girl—Olivia—in my class. She used a braille machine when the rest of us were writing in our journals. Her aide would tell her what was written on the chalkboard and she'd click on this cumbersome typewriter-looking machine. One day when the aide wasn't there, our teacher asked me to work with Olivia. The teacher said my job would be to read out loud to Olivia the notes that were written on the board. After we were done, Olivia let me touch the page she'd taken out of the machine. She asked me, *Can you read that?* When I told her I couldn't, she said, *Well, that's okay, I can't read what's written on the board.* I thought that was great of her to say, kind of a lighthearted way of making sure I didn't feel bad about not being able to read braille. By saying that, she created a connection between us. But Olivia must have moved or changed schools because I haven't seen her since that year. I wonder how much of the time she feels misunderstood. If you can't see at all, how do you ever get oriented in the world? To tell you the truth, I understand that feeling pretty well, even though I can see. Come to think of it, Olivia seemed to see the world better than a lot of other kids.

When I got home from school today, after eating my Fruit Loops, I found a piece of the Hawaiian shirt I put on Fred. I saw a glimpse of it out of the corner of my eye. So, I dug under yesterday's newspaper and found long strips of the shirt. And it looks like Mom ripped the thing into shreds. They were ripped unevenly. I don't have time before she gets home from the store to see if Fred is back in his banker's suit. And this is not the outcome I hoped for when disrobing and redressing Mom's mannequin. I would have thought she'd like to see him more cheerful, brighter, and on the up and up. This, once again, adds to the mystery, the mannequin mystery — the "MM" — but not in a way that seems like it will help me solve anything.

I write back to Peter. I figured it is okay to write straight away since he said so much to me, shared so much with me, in his letter.

Dear Peter,

I got both your letters: the one about King Tut and the one to Mom and me. I didn't know that mannequins had been around so long. I cannot imagine having my own private mannequin. That is amazing. Mom will like the part about Marie Antoinette. She loves French history.

Do you know Morse Code? The package that held the whistle I got last week explains how to send a message with a whistle using Morse Code with short and long whistle blows. Morse code uses dots to mean a quick blow and dashes for a lengthy one. So, if you wanted to whistle FIRE in Morse code, you'd blow two shorts, one long then one short for F followed by one short for I followed by a short /long for R and two shorts for E. That's cool — isn't it?

Mom and I found your books on Amazon. I haven't read too much poetry, except for Langston Hughes and Shel Silverstein. I like Where the Sidewalk Ends.

When's your birthday? Mine is August 9. I'll be 13 this year. I will be an official teenager!

Your pen pal,
Clarence

THE CALLS THAT NEVER COME—SARAH

The last story I worked on writing opens with a man named Thomas standing on the edge of the Golden Gate Bridge prepared to leap off. It's taken him months to get there, to know this is what he needs to do. For longer than he can say he's felt the hurt in his bones, his chest, the place inside him that keeps on rupturing. For years Thomas has been chipping away on a novel called Building A Better Mousetrap about a girl who likes to invent things: mostly devices to ensnare pests — starting with rats and decreasing in size — mice, ticks, fleas, even bedbugs. Then, one day, he gets up the courage to call and read a few sentences of the novel to his sister. He thinks this may be just the thing to help reconnect them as siblings. He also wants to tell her he's dreamed that their mother has started growing hollyhocks because she has heard they can heal the heart. He'll tell his sister that their mother likes the way the Hollyhock flowers are so wide and unwieldy. And that she takes great pleasure in the names of some varieties, names like The Watchman, Queeny Purple, Old Barnyard Mix. What ingenious names, his mother thinks, how whimsical these hollyhocks.

But the phone just rings and rings. Thomas concludes that his sister would have insisted their mother was definitely dead. She would argue that their mother has been dead for over a decade and that it is high time for him to come to terms with that reality. But he's still not 100% sure. He still sees her in line at the bank or at the farmer's market, sometimes the laundromat; public places where it's possible to be indiscernible. Usually she's in the body of a much larger person, sometimes a man in coat and hat, other times a highway worker with a blaze orange vest. But he can always recognize his mother from the way she tilts her head just slightly to the side. At the bank he'll stand and watch as she endorses a check. He remembers so well the way she curved her left hand over her black Flair pen so as not to smudge what words she's already put down. Thomas loves that about her. He loves it more than he can say.

What Thomas is doing on the bridge before he jumps is listing in his head all the words he has found most peculiar. Number one: the letters of his name, spelled backwards, would be samoht which he thinks is a suitable name for an Indian dish. Number two: "ajar." His first car would talk to him — your door is ajar; your door is ajar — if he didn't close it hard enough. And he would rebut, "no, my door is a door, my door is not a jar." Number three: palindromes, words that read the same backwards as forward — "madam", "race-car", "level", "Hannah", and his favorite, "was it a cat I saw". Before my character jumps, he sings *Down in the valley, the valley so low, hang your head over, hear the wind blow.* It was the song his mother sang to him almost every night of his childhood.

I started working on the story after listening to an NPR interview featuring a suicide hotline volunteer. When the NPR interviewer asked, *what do you say at the beginning of the call?* The hotline volunteer explained that he tries to find out the person's location. He tries to keep the caller on the phone as long as he can, ideally until someone can get to him or her. He tries to get the caller through the night. The more specific the plan the caller has for ending their life, the more he worries. The volunteer closed the story by establishing, *the worst calls are the ones that never come.*

FOSSIL HILL—CLARENCE

Last summer I went to an overnight camp for a week. All the kids there were "on the spectrum," but it's not something you would have known. Mom told me she thought it would make me feel more understood to have this week with kids who were more like me. I was pretty scared about going as I had never even spent the night away from home, but I could tell this was something she really wanted me to do, something she'd saved up money for me to do.

I'll tell you some highlights of the camp. There was no pool, so we swam in a river. During swimming hour, there was a buddy system which meant you had to keep your buddy in sight the entire time you were in the water. When they wanted, the counselors would yell "buddy check" and if you didn't hold up your buddy's hand above the water—like an Olympic athlete who's just won a gold medal—by the time they counted to ten, you and your buddy would have to sit out on a bench for ten minutes. It added an extra level of excitement to the entire thing because you most definitely did not want to ever be a bench sitter. And thankfully, I never was.

We also did archery and had to wear leather arm protectors on the inside of the arm we weren't pulling the bow with. I'm right handed, so I had the leather sleeve on my left arm. Despite that, the inside of my arm still got pretty bruised from where the bowstring hit when I released it. I told myself it wasn't happening, though. I told myself it didn't hurt. I can do that if I really put my mind to it, if I really want to keep on going with an activity. And I loved archery. I loved the way the arrow, hitting a fresh target, would make this loud thwack sound, like you'd accomplished something worthwhile: thwack. Plus, I enjoyed seeing what I'd just done so clearly spelled out before me in numbers. And if you got a bullseye, that was like an instant party, an immediate reason to celebrate: bullseye! In that week, I got three.

When it rained and we couldn't do whatever outdoor activity was in store for us, the counselors would crowd us into the dining hall. It was a long, wooden building with screens for windows so the water from the metal roof sounded closer and like it was inside where we were. As the afternoon wore on, the counselors would arrange us in lines along the benches and we played this game where we made a thunderstorm. The first kid in line would rub his hands together — like how you do when you want to get rid of something sticky — and the next kid would do the same, and the next kid, and the next until a loud shushing filled the room. That was the soft rain. Then we'd snap our fingers, one of us and then the next and the next to make it sound like the heavier rain was coming. Then we clapped our hands to make it like rain moving forcefully over the mountain. We'd end up all stamping our feet, and the sound was so loud and close it really seemed like an indoor storm. It was so real.

The very best part of the camp was a barren dirt hill called Fossil Hill. The counselors told us to wear our oldest pair of jeans because we'd be sliding down on our butts — they used that word butts. The hike to Fossil Hill was a little over a mile on a path worn through pastures with cows grazing, all of them facing in the same direction. Then, bang, Fossil Hill just popped up out of the pasture like it was planted there. And boy, was it steep and tall. In order to climb to the top — so we could slide down on our butts — we followed this narrow, switch-backed trail other campers must have made over the years. Once at the top we took turns sliding on pieces of cardboard to the bottom of the hill. As you slid down, your hands would grasp hold of small rocks, some sharp, others pretty well worn. Whatever rocks we had in our hands at the bottom were ours to keep. The counselors explained that if we were lucky, we might find a fossil of a snail or a fish — thousands and thousands of years old. And guess what? I found one! It looks like a feather but is most likely — my counselor said — a fish's tail. I keep it on my dresser. I like to pick it up and turn it over in my hand, sometimes thinking about how all this land around us used to be under water. If one fossil can reveal that truth, then I know that one day I will discover something that will uncover the secret about my dad. I am just going to be patient until that day comes.

First day of camp we played Get-To-Know-You Bingo. This is a game that involves getting the initials of a camper or counselor who fits the criteria written on each bingo square on a sheet of paper such as: someone who can roll their tongue, someone who is left handed, someone willing to stand on one leg and sing the first verse of *Row, Row, Row Your Boat*. It's like a scavenger hunt, but with the people who are all around you. One thing that I discovered is how common the name Robert is. Of the kids in our camp unit, four had it as a middle name: Thomas Robert Cook, Evan Roberts Parton, John Robert Hartford and Lance Robert Lacy. Lance was nice. He was willing to do the stand-on-one-leg-and-sing for me. I did pretty well in the game. The only square I had left blank was *Someone who plays the trombone.*

WHAT THE WHALES ARE SAYING—CLARENCE

Our science teacher, Ms. Sprolini, wears these super long skirts made of what must have been blue jeans, with double stitching and all. It even says Wrangler on the tag. I've never seen her ankles because the skirts drape over her shoes in this way that worries me she might trip. Well, here's the thing: she loves, loves, loves whales. She talks about them all the time in class when I know we are actually meant to be studying cell walls or phases of the moon. The classroom is plastered with whale posters—the Humpback, the Blue, the Killer—and these posters are all loaded with facts about whale behavior and size. So, I now have a lot of information about whales. You can ask me what you want about whales, and I can pop out the answer.

Did you know that forty years ago the Blue Whale—which is the largest animal on earth—was nearly hunted into extinction? Luckily, a bunch of people got together and rallied against killing them. Ms. Sprolini says those people are her heroes. For almost the entire class this past Friday, we listened to whale songs. She put on a CD recorded underwater and asked us to close our eyes, put our heads down on our desks and listen—just like when we were in trouble in first grade, but this felt good. Then she had us write in our science notebooks what we thought the whales were saying. At the end, we shared.

One kid said the whales were playing a game of chess: check, checkmate, check. Evan said it sounded like a soccer game, with all the clicks. My guess is that they were telling each other where the best fish were: *Hey, I found a school of mackerel; everybody swim over here so we can have a feast together.* Truth be told, the whales sound like they are moaning, with a long, low cry. It's kind of sad. But I didn't want to share that and put a damper on the whole whale song party.

Guessing what animals are saying is tricky business. There's no actual way to know you're right. But if you think of it, it's even harder to know what people are thinking. If someone says they're wondering how Doritos are made, they might actually be considering how turtles manage to drink, given the fact that they have a shell on their back that keeps them stiff absolutely all the time. Or they might be considering how some trees lose their leaves in winter while others don't. We just never really can know what someone else is thinking.

ASTONISHMENT—SARAH

The year I taught tenth grade, a boy in my class, Nathan, took his own life. It was astonishing to those of us he left behind. Astonish is the word I use because we hardened a little, stiffened, temporarily turned to stone. It dulled us, stripped of vibrancy. All of us — except for this one boy Robbie, a boy with Asperger's — were silent with nothing useful to say. And while Robbie was a bit of a mystery to me, incessantly brushing his hair with a little yellow hairbrush, it was he who enunciated the formidable truth of what had happened, of what this suicide meant. Just about one week after it happened — we'd just finished reading *Macbeth* — Robbie raised his hand, hairbrush and all, and said Nathan's death was exactly like Macbeth, like someone had taken the life out of the house. He said it in such a nonchalant way, waving that yellow hairbrush like an orchestra conductor. He spoke the truth not one of us had the insight to make. After he spoke those words, our healing began.

And here is another story from a different school, The Putney School, in Vermont. One evening in the dining hall, my colleague's baby choked on a chunk of carrot. The baby was sitting in his highchair, not breathing. His mother picked him up and held him over her shoulder and patted his back gently. But the baby just kept getting redder and redder in the face. For a moment, the entire dining hall fell silent and watched this baby not breathing. Then a kid from the next table got up, pulled the baby from his mother's arms, turned him upside down and thumped him on the back. Out came that carrot. We all clapped and clapped, uproarious and jubilant. Most of us were wiping away tears. What a bold move to take the baby from his mother like that. I remembered all this yesterday after I heard on the radio that Henry Heimlich, at 96 years old, used his own maneuver, the Heimlich maneuver, on another resident at the Cincinnati nursing home where he lives, and it was the first time he'd ever actually performed it.

FOR A LIMITED TIME ONLY—CLARENCE

Advertisements try to get you all worked up by making grand—and often misleading— statements about the product they want you to buy. Plus, the prices are intentionally skewed, so you think a thing is less expensive than it actually is. Something that's priced at $7.89 is most definitely going to be more than $8.00 after you've added in the tax. I guess advertisers hope the number seven will be the resounding number in your head. They hope to get you hooked, get you to think it's a bargain because it's only seven and not eight. So, I have made it my practice to always go ahead and round everything up. That way I'll be sure never to get stuck without enough money.

We should be mighty careful to recognize the catch in the phrase *for a limited time only*. I mean, all time has limits. We don't live forever. There simply is no such thing as limitless time. So how can you say that what is already limited is limited? For a limited time only is a real scam phrase, one you need to be most wary about. When I walk to Wayside Shopping Center, I only ever bring two weeks' worth of allowance. It's part of my savings plan.

The way I see it, we should savor all parts of what we buy. We should enjoy more than the eating or wearing of something we have gotten. We should take full advantage of the entire experience. Because of this, I've taken up the practice of calling companies. Here's an example: written on the bag of my favorite kind of potato chips— Vickie's Chips, barbecue flavored—is the following offer: *If you like our chips call 1-800-VICKIES*. So, I did just that. Well, the lady who answered the phone at Vickie's Chips was nice. She asked what I liked about the chips, asked if she could write down what I said, asked how old I was. Then she offered to mail me a coupon for a free bag of chips, which I did. After the experience with Vickie's Chips, I called the number on the back of my Lucky Charms box. And they just straight out offered to mail me some sample boxes of the cereal. They were such an unusual size, halfway between an actual box and one of those mini boxes that come in variety packs. Mom makes me check in with her before I make these calls, but I think she finds it pretty cool. Just think of all the opportunities out there.

CONCUSSION—CLARENCE

Last winter, during basketball practice, I got bumped by another kid who was doing a lay-up. I landed smack dab on my back and my head hit the hardwood. As I lay on the gymnasium floor, my teammates looked like they had suddenly grown extra limbs and extra heads. Everything kind of doubled right before my very eyes. And I was pretty sure I would throw up, which I'm glad didn't happen right there in front of everybody. Coach helped me up and even though it was nearly the end of practice, he asked the assistant coach to call my mom. When she came, it shocked me to hear the tone in Coach's voice. This guy who is almost always the picture of calmness — "unflappable" Mom calls him — sounded worried. He said, *You might want to take him to the hospital to get him checked out.*

She must have voted against the night-time hospital visit because all I remember is how Mom kept on coming into my room like every hour and waking me up. First thing next morning — instead of school — she took me to see Dr. Taylor. His shoes have a seam that runs across the toe with these perfectly circular indentations. That's what I focused on while he asked me a whole slew of questions. He asked me to say the months of the year in reverse. And, though I can do it now — December, November, October, September — all I could drum up in Dr. Taylor's office was March. So, I said, *March, March, March* like six times in a row. Then he recited a series of five numbers, 8, 13, 2, 95, 7 and wanted me to repeat it backwards. Well, that most certainly would not happen. When he asked me to stand with my right foot directly in front of my left, I tipped over just like a person learning to ice skate. Mom popped up from her chair to catch me. The doctor suggested we go on to the hospital to get an MRI. This is the part that gets even more blurry. I really remember nothing about it. But I can report that if I ever have to go to the hospital again, I want to make sure I have on socks. It is freezing in those places.

All that day and well into the next, the entire world was stunningly bright, even though it was raining outside. When we got home, Mom put our blue, inflatable mattress in her closet, then fixed me a plate of my favorite snacks: pieces of pepperoni really meant for pizza, and pickles, and saltine crackers. She said the doctors needed me to stay in an unlit place so my brain could rest enough to heal from the concussion. But she didn't fully close her closet door, so I could spot Fred's case under her bed. I was thinking how Fred was in his case folded up and I was in her closet, which is a box too. We were both boxed in, quasi hiding, waiting for someone to let us out.

On day two of closet living, Mom caught me staring at the case. And out of the blue she asked me if I had put the shirt on Fred. She said she had wanted to talk to me about it, but just hadn't had the chance to do so yet. At first, I felt caught, but then I got up some courage. *He seemed too drab and plain*, I explained. *And I thought that shirt might cheer him up.* She nodded in a way that said everything was a-ok. And then I asked her, *Whose shirt was it, anyway?* After an endless pause, she said in a low voice, *It belonged to your father.* She said those five words and then turned and walked out of the room. If my head had not been spinning already, it sure was then.

To get my mind off that interaction, I listed words in my head. I like the word jigsaw, how it's both a tool that carpenters use and a kind of game, a puzzle. Plus, a tool really is, at heart, a way to solve a puzzle. A tool can solve a problem — like fixing a toaster or opening a can of baked beans — and a puzzle is a problem. Truth be told, I'm not much good at puzzles. I can reliably get the side pieces, but then the picture on the box and the actual pieces all blur together — those puppy dogs in their basket, the lighthouse by the ocean, the photo of The Golden Gate Bridge — become just one big mass of color with no order to them. But what I love about puzzles is how you always get another chance. You can try one piece, see if it fits, maybe spin it clockwise. If it doesn't fit, well, you just set it down and pick up another piece with vaguely the same color scheme. As far as I can tell, this is not the case in real life. Think of what happens if you board the wrong school bus at the end of the day. Let's say you're paying no attention, have your mind on the math homework sheet you mistakenly left on your desk. You sit down and are busy watching clouds float across the sky through the bus window. Next thing you know you find yourself in a different and unknown neighborhood — or worse, you ride the bus all the way back to school alone where they have to call your mother to come get you.

ANONYMOUS PLACES—SARAH

How do we know if the choices we've made were the right ones? Just how do we know? Yesterday was a brutal one. It hit me smack in the face I'm living a life that is pretty much just a lie. By not telling Clarence the truth of what I do for work and the more important truth of who his father is, I'm making a life for us that is just a veneer. And how do I get out of that one? I am stuck and can't get out of this trap I've made. The knowledge of this descended on me suddenly, and I found myself in the car heading, once again, to Walmart. The only places I feel good lately are Walmart and Kroger. I can wander the aisles pretending to look at blenders or bath towels. I can make myself believe, at least for a bit of time, that I will buy the set of yellow towels and that will be the trick to beginning a new and more honest life.

You know how cars require inspection once a year? Well, maybe people should too. I have no clue who would conduct these inspections, but it would be a way to take a hard look in the mirror, to take stock and inventory of what's working and what's not. If I'm doing better in the aisles of Walmart than anyplace I can think of, then it's a sure bet I would not pass a twelve-point inspection.

Even my best friend from high school has moved on with her life and seems to have no space for me. She stopped returning my calls. She lives in Los Angeles now, with her husband and two daughters, blond girls with perfectly round faces I see in their yearly Christmas card her husband's law firm sends out automatically. I've written her three letters, all asking her to tell me what I did wrong and to make amends. And still she won't write me back.

I hate Christmas cards, the way they portray families as perfect and occupied in interesting endeavors. It makes me so sad because there is no way life can be like that for long. Only one day, for one photo, and then it's all over. I think that's why I hate holidays, days laden with expectations. You are meant to be a certain way, eat turkey and the traditional side dishes, give your dad a new shaving set. It's just too predictable, too programed, when life most definitely is not.

The things Clarence says seem wiser to me than the vast majority of wise aphorisms. He seems to have a handle on things. He sees the world for what it is and is not unsettled by it. Who are we to diagnose one another? In some ways it's useful to have a label, but in another way it's just pigeonholing something, a human life, that is actually far more complex. I know it's meant to be helpful, to have this diagnosis, but sometimes it just hurts and ostracizes. A diagnosis is just a best guess. Who are we to say we know what another person "has"? Even that word "has" seems inaccurate to me. You don't have a disease or a disorder. It has you.

MYSTERY MAIL—CLARENCE

Once a week, usually on Tuesday, a big fat manila envelope comes in the mail for Mom. Inside are invoices for paper towels, toilet paper, sponges, toilet bowl cleaner, Spic & Span. Written on the bottom of each one is "Invoiced to First Baptist Church". That's the enormous church on the corner of Main and 9th street. The day these papers arrive, Mom sits at the kitchen table and inspects each one, then puts a check mark next to the amount—30 rolls of paper towels, check; ten bottles of toilet bowl cleaner, check. When she's all done with the checking, she folds the almost translucent pieces of pink paper back up and returns them to their envelope. It's clear she's concentrating hard while doing all this, almost like it's a job or something, so I don't want to say anything then. Later, she puts the envelope in her purse as if she will take it somewhere. It seems like just when you feel you might get close to solving one mystery, another one crops up. They say you're never too old to learn. I guess I shouldn't be surprised to find more things I don't know about as I get older.

Here's an example: more often than not people you haven't met turn out to differ from what you thought they'd be. You'll have heard a ton about the basketball coach for the upcoming season, how great he is, how he's demanding, but really cares about all the kids on his team. Then, on the first day of practice, he's got blond hair, rather than the dark brown you'd pictured him with. And he isn't even wearing the right kind of shirt for a coach. He's wearing a button down, just without a tie. Talk about having to change your expectations. The thing I've learned to do is not have any real thoughts about people before I meet them. That way I can't be disappointed. Mom says if you don't get your expectations up, they can't get let down.

I used to spend a lot of time imagining who my father was. One week I'd have him look just like me, but in a taller version. The next I'd make him real stocky, the kind of guy you want to hug and play games with. Every few weeks I'd invent for myself a new dad. But I've given up this practice. It seems to have little chance of producing a good outcome.

Back when I was in fourth grade, I even went so far as to write an essay for school about this made-up dad. I turned it in and everything. This, as you might suspect, did not have a very good outcome. My teacher called Mom, and we had a conference about following instructions and telling the truth. The assignment was to write a two-page real story — single spaced — called *The Story of My Life*. It was meant to be a true story. It was meant to be the truth. Here are the first paragraphs about my made-up dad.

The Story of My Life by Clarence James Clark

I still remember the day my dad surprised me with two goldfish. He brought them home in a clear plastic bag that was blown up like a balloon. The bag was filled halfway with water, halfway with air. I loved those fish, named them Eenie and Meenie. It gave me an excuse to hope for more, hope that someday I would get two more fish which I'd name them Mighty and Mo. Unfortunately, and sadly, on day nine of fish ownership, I came home from school to find Eenie and Meenie floating at the top of their perfectly round bowl, just floating on top of the water almost like they were sunbathing or something. But they were dead.

About a week after the death of my goldfish, my dad and I went fishing. We caught some small lake fish but put them back. But we also caught some tadpoles and salamanders my dad said I could keep. My dad is a very fun person and likes to do outdoor activities, but he gets strict with manners and watching television, only half an hour a day.

The essay went on kind of like that, explaining about the manners. But I won't bore you with it all since my fourth-grade writing wasn't that great. Interestingly, the powwow with my teacher and Mom ended up okay. They both said it was wonderful to have a powerful imagination, but that it was important to follow directions and tell the truth. I didn't get into any real trouble, just had to write the essay over. But I did keep the first one, the one about my dad. I have it in my sock drawer along with my allowance. Somehow it seems, at least to me, to have that kind of value. Mom said, out of the blue, that not all dads are fun and like to do outdoor activities. She said I should keep that in mind.

HOW TO DELIVER BAD NEWS—CLARENCE

What if you took everything inside your head and made it so other people could see it? It would be a bit like a television but without all the commercials. Usually I can't explain what's on my mind. It makes me want my own private runaway truck ramp. Have you seen those? On the right side of steep highway stretches sometimes they'll be a sand filled lane that the trucks can safely drive up and decrease in speed and stop in case their brakes fail. That's what I need once I get started explaining to someone how I really feel. It's like my talking brake gave out, and I'm careening out of control saying things I don't mean in any way, shape or form. I just need a sand pit to stop me before things get any worse.

I got my fifth letter—actually a manila envelope this time—from Peter:

Dear Clarence,

You will not believe this, but my birthday is August 10. I was born in 1943, and if my math is correct, you were born in 2003. That means we were born sixty years and one day apart.

I know little about Morse Code, but am in awe of the ability to communicate using only patterns of short and long sounds and of the people who can write down what is being said after only listening to the beeps. Think about all the important messages that have been transmitted that way, Lincoln's declaration ending slavery being one. And that was, without a doubt, a miraculous and important message.

It's been raining for days on end here in St. Louis; the Mississippi River is almost spilling over her banks. While I like the sound of rain, it can get tiresome, having to haul an umbrella everywhere you go. Plus, Linus really hates the rain, looks at me like I'm personally responsible for it whenever I take him on his walks.

I send along my most recent poetry book, Fictitious Force. I hope you and your mom like it.

Your pen pal,
Peter

This letter took my mind off Mom's mystery mail from the church and gave me something to think about: Morse Code. That was a much gentler way of transmitting dreadful news. First, there was nothing casual about a Morse Code message. You wouldn't go to the bother of sending one to say what's up, dude. This manner of communicating was for important matters. Plus, if you were the one reading the code message — if you were the telegraph receiver — you would progressively, beep by beep, recognize and put together what was being transmitted over the wires. That way, it became less jarring. You are already poised to learn something of magnitude, and it comes at you slowly. Seems a lot better than a text message or voice mail that just goes "bam" — here are the facts, deal with them. Maybe we should bring back Morse Code and use it for the heaviest of news.

Why did Peter call the Mississippi River a she? I'll have to ask him about that in my next letter. Speaking of the river, our river freezes almost all the way over in the winter. It's hard to explain just how cold it is here in Rolla seven months out of the year. More than the cold is the wind that blows off the Ozarks. It undoes any cold protection you've arranged for yourself, whips through even two down jackets if you can manage to zip one on top of the other. The absolutely worst part is how your eyes water the second you step outside, tears literally freezing on your cheeks.

It's March now, so the weather's softening. Feels like someone has ironed out all the wrinkles in a piece of cloth. All the ripples and folds are gone, and it's smooth and luscious both at once. After school, I get on my bike. It still fits this year, even though I've definitely grown at least two inches since summer. I like to ride all through the campus of

Missouri University of Science and Technology, zip by students going to afternoon classes.

I find it strange how we say *I'm fine* even when we're not. The day Mom's best friend stopped talking to her for reasons I still can't understand, I suggested we go to Sal's to get some pizza, hoping that might cheer her up. When Antonio, the owner, came up to our table and asked her how she was, Mom said fine. I knew full well she was about as far from fine as she'd been in a while. I think it's the same way that a single lit streetlight in winter is lonelier than no light at all.

NIGHT RADIO—SARAH

There's a midnight show on AM radio I listen to when I can't sleep. I let myself believe that if this host is up, if he is awake, it must be okay that I am too. We're both up in different places but connected through the radio waves. And he uncannily ends up saying things in a way that implies he knows what I need. He's talking directly to me. It's at least a bit of company and the steadiness of his voice (seems always to be a man on these shows) reminds me of my father. Calm and steady, he could say things in a way that would persuade you to do most anything. He even made a dish of ham with pineapple sound like it was something worth eating.

SOME THINGS CAN'T BE TAKEN BACK—CLARENCE

That's what Mom says when I feel tempted to say something mean. She is, of course, talking about taking back words, not items to a store. Those you usually can return. But once you've said something, there's nothing you can do or say that will erase the fact that you've said it. Your statement echoes to many ears, grows bigger over time. It took me awhile to realize the truth of this, but now that I do, I try my best to not have that terrible feeling again of wanting to unsay something. And believe it or not, I have found it easier to let go of some mean things that have been said to me because those who said them may want to take them back, if not at the time, then one day.

Before you go camping, you need to know this trick: dip the heads of your matches in the melted wax of a lit candle so you have that wax as extra protection to keep your matches dry and to help you light a campfire. This is not unlike how it is to be careful with what you say. Put a little wax on things, a smooth coating, and you won't have to worry about being able to create some light and warmth in the world.

Even though I'm way too old for them now, I still love those activity pages that ask you what object does not belong in a picture. There will be a drawing of a typical office and everything in the picture will be office appropriate—computer, telephone, bulletin board, you get the idea. Except secretly lurking in the picture will be a parrot and a piano, or a fishing rod and a wishing bone. When I've found those mis-placed objects, I feel kind of like I've won a race. It's euphoric—this week's word.

Thomas, who is in shop class with me, is short, like half a foot shorter than the rest of us. It doesn't seem to bother him one bit, though. He compensates for it magnificently, puts his tools on the shelf below the table where we work at the beginning of class. Boom—there they are within easy reach. When we were working on our race car project, I tried to always work near him because he'd have what we needed right there in no time at all, and he was more than willing to share.

What if someone just gave up growing? What if Thomas did? Maybe he said *the heck with this, I like the size I am.* Got to admire him a lot if that is what he did. Talk about a free spirit. And I sure am glad I never, ever said anything to him about his height. That would be non-take-away-able. And now we are friends.

OPPOSITES—CLARENCE

The opposite of a vacuum is a blow drier. The opposite of empty is full. The opposite of joy is fear—not sadness. But is freezing the opposite of burning? They feel so much alike. And I don't think the opposite of wanting is having. Do all things have opposites? What is the opposite of dreaming? Gets my head spinning to consider these things, but I think they are important. Is the opposite of digging a ditch building a fortress wall? I just don't know.

Here's how you remember what order the planets are in: by the first letter in each word of the sentence, *My very excellent mother just served us noodles.* So, you can always remember Mercury, Venus, Earth, Mars, Jupiter, Saturn, Uranus, and Neptune. In science we're learning how to classify living organisms. You can use the sentence *King Philip came over for good spaghetti* to remember kingdom, phylum, class, order, family, genus, and species.

Today we learned about this bird called the Masked Booby who lives in the Galapagos Islands where it's blazing hot and the sun is enough to eat you alive. If the female Masked Booby gives birth to twins—which happens 30% of the time—the siblings fight and one of them dies. Now, that seems harsh. I prefer not to think too long on that one. So, on a related topic, here is some good news: crickets can pretty accurately tell us the temperature. This is only the case in summer when crickets are out and about. But here's how it works: if you count the number of times a cricket chirps in 15 seconds, add 37 to it, you will be close to what the temperature is outside. Try it next time you hear a cricket. I even keep a record of it taped to the refrigerator. When I remember, I record a minute of a cricket's chirping, do the math, then write down both the actual temperature and what the crickets say the temperature is. Usually they are mighty close, if not the exact same.

CHASING MY OWN SHADOW: CLARENCE

Meemaw died. We found out about it over the phone. Uncle Dave called to tell us. Mom kind of stiffened when she heard his voice on the phone. And I could tell that something inside Mom was permanently changed as she heard what her brother had to say. She barely spoke, said yes a few times and okay twice. She thanked him for calling and said she'd wait to hear about plans. Then she hung up. She just hung up the phone in silence, slowly.

Witnessing this phone call was like watching someone become a different person before your very eyes. Prior to the phone call, she was someone's daughter. After it, she was not. It took Mom a few minutes to tell me, even though I knew what she was about to say. But this is how she put it: *Buddy, Meemaw had a heart attack. She died this afternoon on the way to the hospital.* The whole time Mom was saying this, I couldn't keep myself from thinking how I used to chase my shadow. We would be out at recess, on the blacktop, and I believed that if only I tried hard enough, I'd catch the shape of myself. So, I'd lurch forward, trying to get away from my real self and into the shadow I saw. Somehow this feels the same as learning Meemaw died.

When I was little Mom would turn up the music real loud — some song like *Big Rock Candy Mountain* — and we'd dance in the kitchen, me standing on her feet so we'd become two people with one set of legs. As I got taller, we figured out how we could hold hands and find balance while dancing to *There's a land that's fair and bright where the handouts grow on bushes and you sleep out ev'ry night.* I remember how clean she smelled, like we ourselves were made of candy there in the kitchen dancing as one.

I read a few poems from Peter's book. It's quality stuff. Mom took the book to her room, so she must be reading it back to front. This is the letter I wrote to him.

Dear Peter,

I like it that we have the almost-same birthday. That's what I will call it, the almost-same.

I've read a few poems from your book. I think Fictitious Force is a splendid title. Scientific terms do an outstanding job of summing up complex, hard-to-understand things. I looked up fictitious force: every action has an equal and opposite reaction. That's a cool idea. Other scientific terms I like are boiling point — which is the temperature at which water turns to vapor — and spontaneous combustion, even though I'm not sure I understand what that one is. Can you explain it?

This year science is definitely my favorite subject. Our teacher says that questions are actually more important than answers, and incorrect answers teach us as much as — if not more than — correct ones. This makes me happy because if you think about it, we're bound to be wrong at least half the time.

Got some new stamps, this one is of Louis Armstrong. We studied him in history.

Can you tell me why you called the Mississippi River a she?

Your pen pal,
Clarence

THE HAZARDS OF UMBRELLAS—SARAH

I've never understood the reasoning behind umbrellas. I get that they are intended to be a mini roof over your head and prevent you from getting wet. But the two obstacles — wind and potential for eye poking — far outweigh the benefits in my mind. There are few more disconcerting sights than a broken, abandoned umbrella, turned inside out, spokes bent the wrong way. You relive the moment in your mind, how it must have been a driving, windy rain, how the umbrella's owner got soaked and frustrated and just left the darned thing there. Why not opt for a practical, yellow raincoat? Additionally, umbrellas are antisocial. I mean, have you ever really successfully shared an umbrella with someone? You walk out of a building in an unexpected April rain and your workmate offers, *come get under the umbrella with me*. Well, you don't both walk at exactly the same pace and the thing is not really big enough for two, so it's just downright awkward. I read somewhere that military personnel may not use umbrellas when in uniform. That makes perfect sense to me.

I'm not sure why I'm so adamant about or feel the need to even bring up the subject of umbrellas. I guess one of my life's ambitions is to give equal credence to feelings. Our world is so enthralled with facts that the realm of feeling is most often passed over as lighthearted, regarded as frivolous. And I would like to change that. I would like to help the world see that what we feel, how we feel, is equally — if not more — vital than provable facts.

THE HALF LIFE OF MAGNIFICENCE—CLARENCE

Mom is super good at finding what we need at the Goodwill store. The one in Rolla's big, and they organize everything according to color. When we go, I usually beeline it back to the electronics section. In the past year alone, I've scored three times: a lava lamp that worked perfectly, a CD player that also had a place for cassette tapes—which Mom likes because some of her lectures from college are on those tapes. And then, the week after Christmas, there was a brand new—still in the box—Razor scooter. Don't know what it was doing in electronics, but I snatched that one up. It was only $5.00.

Today when we went to Goodwill, there was a guy playing a piano. The piano was to the right of the entrance as soon as you walked into the store. It looked really beat up, coffee rings on the top, some of the wood chipped, you get the picture. But this guy made that piano sound amazing. It's like he brought it back to life, made it wake up. So, there I was pretending to be interested in women's jackets beside Mom—who was interested in women's jackets—and listening to the triumphant sound this guy was making on the piano. I could tell Mom was impressed too, but neither of us wanted to ruin the moment by saying anything about it. You know how that is. Saying something about a great thing kind of takes its power away, cuts its magic in half. That is the half-life of magnificence. And none of us wants to be guilty of that. Well, after piano player finished, I heard, from behind the curtain that separates the back of the store, one Goodwill worker say to another: *The piano's going, thank God. The customer who was playing it will pick it up tonight at 5:30.* Well, I am glad the maestro got his piano at the Goodwill. There is no half-life to a gift like that, to turning something discarded into something great.

Yesterday after school, Mom took me to the bank to open my own bank account. She said I was old enough to have one, and it would be an excellent way for me to learn about money. She said if I keep all my money in one place, I might have a better chance of saving up for something I really want. I get five dollars a week for allowance. I usually have at least a dollar left over, which I stick in an envelope underneath my socks. Also, sometimes when I'm hanging out at Rent-to-Own Larry will ask me to move a bunch of pillows out of the way or to help him move small pieces of furniture, like end tables or lamps. After I do that, he'll hand me a couple dollars. One day, I even rearranged the entire back of the store, and he gave me ten dollars. So, I have—and this surprised Mom—one hundred and forty-three dollars and seventy-eight cents.

We went to Bankers Trust, waited in the normal line to see a teller who told us to have a seat and a banker would be with us shortly. I love it when people use the word "shortly" when what they mean is a short amount of time. But shortly sounds so much like shorty all I can picture is a midget coming out to meet us.

Eventually—not shortly—this guy named Al told us to come with him to his glassed-in cubicle. There were two chairs close to each other on one side of the desk. Al wedged himself into a black chair with roller wheels. Right away I picked up that this guy was nervous. He kept jiggling his leg like there was a fly on it he needed to get rid of. When he asked what must have been a second time for my middle name, and I said I don't have one, his leg stopped jiggling. He bent over the form and wrote *Clarence Clark*, leaving the middle name space blank. Truth be told, I do sort of have a middle name. It's James. Mom says there's a river in Virginia called the James that is wide and lovely and hopeful. That's why she made it part of my name. But I never see her write it on any of the forms she has to fill out at school or at the doctor's office. When I asked her about this omission, I could tell that question was not one she wanted to hear. It was not one she wanted to answer. So, I vowed to leave it alone and consider James to be my secret middle name.

FAMOUS LAST WORDS—SARAH

Tracing my grandmother's hands was a habit. The times we went to visit her on the little island where she lived, I could feel my mother tense up, tighten, shut down even more.

Thinking about it now I see it was an amazing transformation: my mother, already self-contained, reticent and taut, becoming even more closed in when in the presence of her own mother. And I suspect she resented the way my grandmother took to me, writing me letters on her fine cotton Crane's stationery every week, setting out a crystal bowl of Hershey's kisses in the hallway when we'd visit. I'd sit beside her at the kitchen table, ask her to lay her palms flat, and trace their shapes in crayon. Then I'd color them in, make islands with five peninsulas, draw in miniature houses and trees. The one time we stayed overnight, I made a village square in her palm, even colored in the stained-glass windows of the church, including a sign outside the grocery advertising a sale on Yukon gold potatoes and corned beef hash. Looking back, I see these drawings of my grandmother's hands were my way of joining in the conversation, which almost always ended with great disappointment and strife.

Even though my relationship with my mother was at times corrosive, I loved her very much. More than love, even, was my great respect for her, a burgeoning feeling of gratitude for how she made do and got through each day which was, without a doubt, a burdensome task for her. Being alive was plain and simply difficult for her. Each loomed ahead of her, large and foreboding.

When David called me to say our mother had died, I was in the bathroom flossing my teeth, taking care to get between every tooth the way the dental hygienist has showed me, trying to mimic the way the hygienist made it seem as if it's the easiest thing in the world to do, when actually it's tricky. I am concentrating on teeth cleaning, and

Clarence picks up the phone in the kitchen, and says *Oh hi Uncle Dave*, but then he does not talk with him. Clarence just comes in to tell me the phone is for me. I remember standing with the cord wrapped around my finger when he said our mother had died, suddenly and painlessly, of a heart attack. She was pronounced dead in the ambulance on the way to the hospital. Because Clarence was listening to my end of the conversation, I knew better than to say much in response, so I thanked him for letting me know. This was directly in keeping with our family's stiff upper lip culture. Then I told Clarence matter-of-factly. Even though he was not that close to Margaret, I didn't want to make him distraught. This was going to be mine to deal with, privately, on my own.

That night, after Clarence fell sleep, I sat and stared out the front window long past dark. As I watched the streetlights come on, I remember thinking of how I was never going to see my mother again, never going to have a chance to tell her about what I am reading. That was the most intimate we ever got, sharing with one another what we were reading. It was mollifying to talk about books, to analyze their characters and describe their settings, as if we were sharing actual places where we had been. We'd report the findings of our reading to each other as if recounting a change in the weather or an accident we'd witnessed. Books were that real.

I am afraid, now, when I finish a book that I will start to dial her number to only then realize I have no one to call and share the book with. A year or two from now, it will happen. Or next week. Either way, I'm quite certain it will, and it will hurt more sharply than I can predict. There is no anesthetic for grief, no ointment, only the hope that one day it will lighten, lift a little, stop pressing down.

In the future if I fall into a spell of missing her too much, I will force myself to remember her cynicism. It will help. She had a habit of putting people into categories and never letting them out. Once you were flighty in her mind, you were never again capable of responsible decisions. You couldn't be trusted. If she found a woman to be vain, she would barely give her the time of day. She had a habit of using the phrase *famous last words* not to conjure up memories of actual words people had uttered before death, but to assert her doubt that a promise would be fulfilled.

If her brother said that he would try to work on being more organized she would say, *Famous last words*. If the plumber promised he'd be timelier next time she called in need of his services, she'd turn to me after he'd closed the door and say, *Famous last words*.

Another aphorism she used with great regularity was *peanuts and past performances*. If someone explained that their great-great uncle was a general in World War One, she'd say, quietly — or not so quietly — under her breath, *peanuts and past performances*. This meant, basically, get off your high horse, it's not you who did that. It meant those past accomplishment are peanuts, are of little value now. I was always secretly fearful that she'd use it in reference to a friend of mine. During college, my friend Mary came home with me for the weekend and wanting to impress my mother, told her she was related to Walt Whitman. I held my breath, utterly terrified that my mother would say to Mary's face *peanuts and past performances*. Luckily, she did not. She waited and told me later in private. But it does make me remember that it was immensely hard to impress my mother. Maybe she'd had so many early impressions with people's vanity, unpleasant ones as a child, that she was not going to let her guard down enough to celebrate another person's accomplishments. That was hard to live with, particularly as a daughter.

ACT LIKE A BEAR'S CHASING YOU—CLARENCE

When you are hiking and come upon a bear, or a bear comes upon you, the given advice is to make yourself look as big as possible. If you are wearing a sweatshirt, you should raise it over your head both high and wide. This will make you look large and powerful in the bear's eyes. If no sweatshirt is available, you should stand on your tiptoes. That does not work as well as the sweatshirt, but it's a next best thing. And here is what not to do when you come upon a bear: do not crouch or run away. Crouching makes the bear think you are poised to pounce. Running alarms the bear, particularly if it's a momma who will definitely chase you. I am not sure I remember who told me all this, and I haven't checked it for accuracy, but it strikes me as being pretty good advice for whenever you feel threatened.

So, if another person is teasing you, make yourself as big on the inside as you possibly can. If someone's trying to bully you, and you've made yourself bigger, the proportion of you that can be hurt is smaller. Does that make sense? If there is more of you, then the percentage of you that is getting hurt decreases. Teachers are all the time talking about bullying. And the next time the subject comes up, I'm going to say, "just act like you would if a bear were chasing you." I will go on to explain my reasoning for the whole thing.

Sometimes dew collects on spider webs, and this makes it so you notice them more. Because the school bus is so much higher off the ground than a car, I am closer to the spider webs that are strung in the air. This morning I spotted a series of webs stretched across the entire expanse between two horizontal power lines. The water from the dew made them look like they were strings of diamonds glittering in the morning sun.

On our bus route, we pass many sketchy sights, but the one that fascinates me most is what I secretly call "The Indecisive House". One day outside the house will be a sign out that reads "For Sale by Owner." The very next day will be a different sign, different color, different handwriting that reads: "For Rent." This has been going on for as long as I can remember. Sometimes it stays for sale for an entire week. So that week it's for sale; but then the next week it's for rent. Today there was no sign whatsoever. Maybe the owner sold it or rented it or just plain gave up.

Lately I've wondered about endings to stories. How in the world does a person know, how is an author 100% sure, that a book is done? It not like a pot roast or basketball game. When a pot roast is done, it's done. When the time is up for a game, and the loud buzzer sounds, it's time to shake the other team's hands and head on home. I am always a little bit disappointed when I come to the last page of a book and the author has even gone so far as to skip an entire line and write "The End" in larger font. In real life, there are so few definite endings. Each ending is really a beginning too. And sometimes with really good books, even though the author writes "The End" after the last line, there will be another book written that picks up exactly where the previous one left off.

Mom used to read me a fairy tale by e.e. cummings. He was a guy who rarely used any capital letters, which is kind of cool if you think about it. Anyway, he wrote this story called *the little girl named I*. It's about this girl who invites a cow to come over to her house for tea. But the cow likes grass, not tea, and looks at the girl with big eyes and says *no thanks*. Next, the girl invites a horse, then a pig, then an elephant, over for tea. But the animals all decline her invitation. Saddened, the girl sits down by a pond, sees her own reflection in the water and asks that girl — who is herself but she doesn't know it — to tea and they have some fine hot tea...along with bread and butter and jam. Then, on a line all by itself, cummings has written *And that's the end of the story*. I don't know about you, but I feel like we need a little bit more. What happened next? Did the girl ever realize she was having tea by herself? Did she stop being sad?

Cummings wrote another story called *The Elephant and The Butterfly*. It begins, *Once upon a time there was an elephant who did nothing all day*. What an honest and straight-forward beginning to a story — nothing like telling the truth as you see it! Well, the elephant lives at the top of this hill with a long winding road going down it. At the bottom of the road lives a butterfly. One day the butterfly comes up the road to elephant's house. And the elephant invites the butterfly in because it's beginning to rain — which, as we all know, is pretty bad news for butterflies. When it stops raining, the elephant puts his arm carefully around the little butterfly and asks *Do you love me a little?* The butterfly waits a moment before answering, *No, I love you very much.* That's a great twist in the story, if you ask me.

ADVICE COLUMN TO MYSELF—CLARENCE

I am fascinated by how people write into the newspaper with their personal problems, and Abby or Ann writes back with an answer. Sometimes Mom even reads the responses out loud to me. If I wrote into an advice column, I would ask Abby or Ann what they think happened to my dad and what I should do about it. I would sign my letter, *Mulling It Over in Missouri*. That way, if I ever sent it, no one would recognize the questioner as me. Anyway, what I'd have Abby say in her response to me would be to never give up, keep on trying, that someday I will find out who my dad is and what has happened to make it so he's not in the picture.

Tomorrow we have a math quiz, but I just straight up know this week's material, so no need to study. But I do have history to finish. We're learning about The Harlem Renaissance, studying all the artists and painters who lived then. Yesterday we listened to Louis Armstrong's music. Most everyone knows his song *It's a Wonderful World*. But he also did this cool thing called scat, which is basically making the noises of instruments with your mouth. He imitates the drums and cymbals so convincingly you can trick yourself into believing he is the instrument. It's hard to stop reading up on someone like Louis. His mother had some pretty sketchy jobs. When he was little, his dad just up and left, got another full-on family, wife and kids, the whole setup. Maybe that's what my dad did, just skipped town when he realized what he was in for. But I'm not giving up. I will keep on trying to figure out who he is or was. Just like my advice column said. Any opportunity I have, any clue I can find, I'll follow it fully until there are no more breadcrumbs to gather.

After I finished my homework, Mom took me to Sam's Hot Dog Stand. Their hot dogs come with all the toppings: onions, relish, mustard and ketchup, and even chili. I usually get the chili and think of it as two meals in one. You have the hot dog meal, plus you have the chili meal — two dinners. They also sell Dippin Dots: yumm. This week they even had watermelon flavored Dippin Dots: super yum.

I love percolators because you can watch what is happening, watch the boiling, the coffee being made. About twice a year mom decides to throw a bit of a breakfast party for just the two of us. Instead of my usual cereal breakfast, Mom joins me on a Sunday morning, and we have eggs, grits, sausage, orange juice, the whole spread. The best part, though, is when Mom gets out the percolator she's had since college and makes her coffee on the stove. She says, *Clarence, it's time,* and that's my cue to assemble what I call "the stomach of the pot", which consists of all these aluminum pieces: hollow tube, a perforated basket and a cap. I put the coffee grounds in the basket after filling the pot with water, then put on the cap and the top to the pot itself. The top has a glass knob on it and once we put the pot on the stove burner, after right around four minutes, the water starts gurgling up into the glass knob. At first, it's almost clear but as the boiling progresses the color darkens: coffee! I have the feeling that if I weren't there she wouldn't even bother with this endeavor, but I watch over it carefully and have a skilled eye for when the color's just right and her coffee is ready. I call these our percolator mornings. We don't talk that much during the preparation part because we're both pretty tied up. She's stirring the grits, adding some cheese at the end, and I'm watching the percolator. But the kitchen is most definitely not silent with the gurgling percolator, the boiling grits, the frying eggs; lots of popping and sputtering. It's an all-around good time. I love the way the windows fog up so it's like we are in our own private chamber with its very own atmosphere.

QUIETER THAN SLEEP—SARAH

We all know there are too many radio shows about Jesus, program hosts trying to tell us what to believe about him, as if they themselves held the secret to it all. I think what bugs me most is how their voices take on this urgent pitch, as if there is a fire and we all must immediately react. It's almost like they are yelling, but they're not. It's actually worse than yelling. If you ask me, I think that what we believe should be the quietest thing imaginable, quieter than breathing, quieter than sleep.

PROBLEMS ASTRONAUTS FACE—CLARENCE

When I was little, I used to think my teachers went into the classroom supply closet after we left school, and that they stayed there until the next day when we came back to school. I was downright frightened if I saw a teacher buying oranges at the grocery store or renting a movie at Family Video. How could they do normal things like that? When I saw Mrs. Adams, my second-grade teacher, at Crafts and Things on the Saturday before Halloween— Mom and I were scouring for supplies to make me into a pinecone— I hid behind the display of scarecrows and stayed there until I saw Mrs. Adams check out and leave the store.

Recently I've have made myself a challenge to try and figure out what kind of car each one of my teachers drives. It's more like an investigation. My Language Arts Teacher, Mr. Miller—begins each class with a few puns and gives out "Smarties" candy rolls if you answer correctly, and "Dum Dum" lollipops if you are wrong. It's all done in jest, so no one feels bad. Well, he drives this ancient red Toyota. The passenger side door is a lighter shade than the rest of the car, and the bottom has entire places missing where there is rust. Boom: that is the exact car I would have thought Mr. Miller would drive. Mrs. Adams drives a Prius, the exact car I would have guessed for her. My art teacher drives a Scion that she must have painted flowers all over herself— perfect.

I got another letter from Peter. These days, I look forward to the mail. Pretty good odds there will be a letter for me. He wrote this one on the inside of a box of Life cereal. He must have taken the box apart pretty carefully as there was not a rip in sight.

Dear Clarence,

Since you mentioned eating different kinds of cereal, I thought I'd write this letter on a box. I eat Life cereal most mornings, sometimes with yogurt, other times plain.

Spontaneous combustion is when an object just catches on fire all by itself. Most often it happens with rags that have been soaked in oil, or hay that has been baled when it is too wet.

As far as your question about the river being a "she", I have to admit I really do not know. I also don't know why people tend to name boats "she". But I will keep searching for answers and let you know if I find one.

I really like your Louis Armstrong stamp. That guy sure could make the trumpet resound. I send you a Joe DiMaggio. He was a great baseball player.

Your pen pal,
Peter

Thinking of Louis Armstrong and Joe DiMaggio gets me back to the topic of possible things to do — or what adults say, "be" — when I grow up. Sometimes as I watch the weather channel on the big screen at Rent-To-Own, I think being a meteorologist might be one sweet job. I've come up with three reasons. Number one: you get to hear before most people about big upcoming storms, tornadoes, hurricanes, and the like. Number two: people tend to pay close attention to anyone who knows something first. Why else would news be so popular? Number three: you are forgiven if you are wrong. You are dealing, after all, with Mother Nature, the all-powerful. Plus, there are those huge touch screens you get to stand in front of and swipe.

Which job would you rather have: chauffeur or pilot? It's a game I play in my mind. Would you rather be a trash collector or a prison guard? Be the person who clicks numbers to count when someone goes into a museum or a TSA worker? On the radio they were talking about how much stress astronauts face. We all know about the freeze-dried ice cream, the absence of gravity — which I personally think would be ultra-cool — and the fact you have to drink your own recycled pee. But there are more lasting physical effects that made me take pause. Sometimes astronauts lose much of their eyesight. And sometimes they get really bad headaches for years and years after a mission. Did you know that astronauts are actually taller in space? Our science teacher explained how, without gravity, the spine lengthens, and this can be painful. Also, because they are free floating rather than walking around, their legs end up getting really weak. And it's extremely hard to sleep because the spaceship is super noisy. When I think of it, though, the hardest part would be coming back to earth. Imagine how strange it would be to come back to streets, and people, and smells, and fresh food, and dogs, and just about all the things we have every day. It would be such a shock, I think you'd want to just hide in a box, one that resembled the inside of an aircraft.

Sometimes I try to remind myself that you can make any job pretty great by tweaking things a bit. Being a mailman could be an awesome job. First off, you'd have real insider information on people who lived in the very town you do. If Rufus Jones subscribed, let's say, to "Field and Stream" you could nonchalantly mention the six-pound catfish you caught at the lake on Saturday next time you see him in line at Kroger. And you might strike up a friendship right then and there. Or if Betty Walsh frequently got packages stamped eBay you could chat her up about the feeling of last minute bidding. People might come to think you are psychic or something.

Also, if you're a door-to-door mail deliverer, you'd never have to worry about going for a morning jog or hitting the gym after work. Those people must walk literally miles and miles every day. But certainly, the very best part would be getting to drive any old way you wanted if you were a rural route delivery person. If a mailbox were on the other side of the road, you'd whip your truck right on over there against the traffic, breaking all manner of laws. You'd leave your truck wherever and however you wanted: two tires up on a sidewalk, in the bank drive thru. That would feel powerful. And this is just one example of a job that at first glance might seem dull but turns out to be quite the opposite. One job I admire is that of an elevator inspector who slides his initialed certificate under the glass frame, knowing, the whole time, that what he's looked over, what he's made sure is safe, will carry people up and down in a dark shaft for an entire year.

One tricky job would be that of being a truck driver. There's a super low train bridge in Rolla — only thirteen feet high — and a few times each year a truck gets stuck. When I was nine, I saw it happen. We were on a field trip with our fifth-grade teacher, Mr. Johnson. We'd walked to the public library and just as we turned the corner where the low bridge is, a tractor trailer came screeching to a halt. It got stuck under the trestle bridge, the top of the trailer having rolled back like the lid of a sardine can. Mr. Johnson let us stop and watch how the truck would get unstuck. At first, I had no idea how in the world that truck would ever get out of there. I kept on thinking and thinking, until I realized I'd been thinking the wrong way, thinking up instead of down. A mechanic came and talked to the truck driver for a few minutes. After that he took what looked like a knife and pressed in the valve of each tire, and the truck went whoosh and lowered about three good inches. For the next month, pretty much any math problem in Mr. Johnson's class had to do with the height of that bridge and the truck's tires. He always made up his own word problems. I liked that about him.

Mr. Johnson also read to us, for at least an hour every single day. He let us lie on the thick blue rug while he sat in a rocking chair, his voice floating over us. By October of that year, a few of us took up the practice of sticking pencils into his cowboy boots while he sat rocking and reading to us. Because he wore his boots outside his pants it was pretty easy to stick a pencil in there without his noticing. The first day we did it he was in the middle of reading *Where the Red Fern Grows* and this kid, Noah, held up a long perfectly sharpened pencil. Then he oh-so-slowly moved closer and closer to Mr. Johnson, inch by inch. Once he was sitting right at Mr. Johnson's feet, Noah simply dropped the pencil in the front part of one of his boots, which were really wide and open at the top. Of course, this was like the best thing ever. The next day three of us brought pencils when it was reading time and passed the pencils up to Noah who became our designated pencil depositor. It wasn't until the third day that Mr. Johnson realized that his boots had half a dozen pencils in them. Or maybe he did notice earlier but didn't let us know. But this is how he said it: *It seems as if pencils have been finding their way into my boots. If you wish to claim your pencil, you may come to my desk during free desk time.* Pretty smooth, I'd say.

Yesterday was The Preakness, and so I went over to Rent-to-Own to watch it on the big screen. Mom was napping. She told me to remember as much as I could about the race in order to recap it for her when I got home. Even though there was what looked like a college student already watching, I sat down in the other La-Z-Boy and said hi. I instantly got the feeling he was pulling for American Pharaoh, just like me. It was raining in Baltimore, droplets of rain showing up on the camera lens, like magnified pearls of water. The reporter explained it was pouring so hard they had cleared all spectators off the course.

For a moment, right before post time, it looked like they were going to delay the race, but they did not. It was incredible to watch the horses running so fast in the mud and pouring rain. The announcer explained that the jockeys had on three, even four, pairs of goggles and would pull off one pair once it got too obscured by the rain. Not sure why I love watching horse racing so much, given that I've barely even seen a horse in real life — once in St. Louis. But it just makes me feel like I'm there, that part of me is the rider, the one racing. I hold my breath almost the whole time, and definitely as they approach the last turn. When American Pharaoh won, the college student and I gave each other a high five. It was a triumphant moment.

I wrote Peter back more quickly this time. Mom and I are planning to go to St. Louis in the next month. She says it's about time for another visit. Even though I haven't yet asked her about meeting up with him, I want to make sure he'll be around.

Dear Peter:

I watched the Preakness today. I went next door where there's a store that rents furniture and stuff and saw it on the big screen. I was rooting for American Pharaoh and am glad he won.

Mom and I are thinking about coming to St. Louis sometime soon. Are you going to be around all spring?

Your pen pal,
Clarence

QUESTIONNAIRE FOR HANSEL AND GRETEL— CLARENCE

Of all fairy tales, I have the most serious reservations about what Hansel and Gretel decide to do. In case you have forgotten, here's a quick summary of the story: Hansel and Gretel are a brother and sister whose evil stepmother tries to abandon them in the woods because she doesn't want to have to feed them anymore. So, in the middle of the night the stepmother takes them far from their home into a dense forest. And Hansel leaves a trail of breadcrumbs in order that he and his sister can find their way home. The breadcrumbs, of course, get eaten before they get back to them. Lost, brother and sister meet a white bird who leads them to a clearing in the woods where there is a cottage made of gingerbread. Hansel and Gretel are really hungry and begin to eat the rooftop and windowpanes. Then, boom, the door opens, and a haggard looking witch comes out and tells them to come inside as she has cozy beds and food for them. But what the witch plans to do is to kill the children. She will fatten them up, then cook them and eat them. When the witch tries to get Gretel to open the oven to put Hansel in, Gretel pretends that she does not understand what she is being told to do. When the witch demonstrates, Gretel cleverly shoves the witch in the oven and she and Hansel are free.

What I want to know is a) why they would think it's okay to eat someone's house b) why they would believe this strange witch and go into her house and c) why they would want to go home after what their wicked stepmother did to them. Seems to me they'd want to stay as far away from her as possible. The only answer I can come up with is that they missed their dad. It's strange how we'll go to pretty extreme measures when we love someone.

I guess the point of Hansel and Gretel is to instruct children in the dangers of running away from home. Guess that's why the story has stayed popular all these years. If you take time to think of it, a lot of fairy tales are really and truly scary. Think of *Little Red Robin Hood*. That's awfully sketchy how the wolf pretends to be her grandmother. And the Three Little Pigs: that one's harsh. The wolf huffs and puffs and threatens to blow the pigs' house down. Maybe someone should write stories for little kids that aren't so frightening.

Did you know that it's impossible to tickle your own self, that the brain doesn't allow it? That would make a cool children's story. I'd entitle it *The Boy Who Learned to Tickle Himself*. And he'd be the only human being ever to succeed at that feat. And this, also, is true: in Malawi children are deemed old enough to go to school when they can touch their ear by reaching their opposite hand over their heads. Instead of going to kindergarten when you are, say, five, they measure you and see if you can reach your hand over your head and get to your own ear. I like that. And I also like the fact that a mannequin cannot wear gloves. Their fingers are glued together so no gloves.

In chess, the queen can move in any direction. Other characters cannot go sideways. Others can only go sideways. I've been thinking about this, even though I don't really know how to play chess, even though I looked all this up on the internet about the game. What if, like crabs, we could only move sideways? What if some of us had the exclusive right to move in a particular way? I was thinking all this today at breakfast, which is the day I started drinking milk with my cereal. Before that I would put the milk in my cereal, but not drink a glass of it on the side. I have to admit I will miss how the cereal kind of colors the milk. It's like it becomes something else. Once Mom bought Pet milk. I thought it was milk from someone's pet cat — but how would that work? I thought about that for a long time.

BLANK MAPS—SARAH

When I was in middle school we would routinely be presented with a blank map: of the United States, of what was then called Russia, of Africa, sometimes of the whole world. And we'd have to write in where everything was. I never did very well. And I still don't. I never seem to be able to parse out in my mind where things belong either literally or figuratively. I tend to navigate the world by insight, more than by fact. The year I taught here in Rolla, my students and I set out to compile a list of agreed upon facts: oil floats on water, if you touch its whiskers a cat will blink, the earth is not flat. But the exercise got tricky really quick. We all had to agree it was an agreed upon fact. What we were talking about relied upon insight. If you look up the word in a dictionary, you will find it to mean perception, acumen. But if you dig deeper you discover that the word comes from the archaic Scottish word "insicht" which means furniture or household goods. Isn't that amazing that insight was once regarded as something we can own, something we do own, like a pair of shoes, a dishwasher, a toothbrush.

SURVIVAL OF THE FITTEST—CLARENCE

Long, long ago giraffes had short necks. Because they eat leaves, those with longer necks were able to get to more leaves, the high up ones. This meant they got enough to eat and lived healthy full lives, lived long enough to have babies. And those babies inherited the longer neck. This went on and on through time. Gradually, over many giraffe generations, the necks lengthened to what we know them to be now. But take a moment to picture a giraffe's head. What in the world are those horns with tufts for? It's as if the giraffes just landed here on a spaceship and are sending messages back to their homeland. And here's what's truly stunning: they have the biggest hearts of any mammal. Plus, even with their long necks they have the same number of vertebrae as we do. It just sets me afloat to think of it all.

Okay, so I have waited this long to tell you, but I have a pretend friend. Liam is not always around, just when I'm feeling extra lonely. He and I mull things over. Today we are wondering what it's like to be a dog, to want little more than food, water, the occasional pat on the head, someone patient enough to take you on daily walks. This makes us think about Darwin and his finches. Did you know that is the animal Charles Darwin, the dude who proved the truth of evolution, used to show survival of the fittest? And I wonder why he chose a slight bird, given all the beasts in the world, to prove a point as significant and world altering as his? Why not something spectacular and imposing? Our science textbook makes things perfectly clear with menacing photographs of stripes on cheetahs, spots on tigers, an amputee's children whose limbs were most definitely intact. There's even a photo of a rabbit to whose back someone'd secured an ice pack, resulting in a permanent bald spot. On the next page: the rabbit's offspring with flawless, sleek, full coats of fur. This makes things darn clear that those with stronger traits will survive and that we adapt to what's around us to do so.

There are bears called okapi bears with stripes. Except for their shape they look a lot like zebras, but, get this, they are most closely related to the giraffe. And they don't even have long necks. How do we even know facts are facts? Because someone says they are? That seems sketchy to me. Maybe this is why it would be good to be a scientist. You'd have evidence to back up a lot of the things swirling through your head.

Did you know that when you chop someone's head off that person can still think and feel for another twenty seconds? We learned this in history when we studied The Reign of Terror and the head chopping off device that's called a guillotine. Historians report that a lady, Charlotte Corday, lifted her head from the basket where it landed and slapped her own cheek. Those watching said she looked really mad. Talk about creepy.

We take a class at school called life skills which is, if you ask me, just a way to tell us about our bodies. But yesterday the subject was jobs. We had to report on what our parents do. The teachers seem to skip over me when this question pops up, so I didn't have to answer. Lara Smith said her dad works as a practice patient. That, of course, peaked everyone's interest. Practice patient—what's that? She explained how he spends three days a week at a hospital in St. Louis where there are medical students learning to be doctors. He is told to act like something specific is wrong with him, like his appendix is killing him or he is having a heart attack. The med student attending to him is graded not only on whether they guess the correct problem—what she said is called an accurate diagnosis—but also on what Lara explained is called bedside manner, which is basically how nice you are to the sick person lying there. That is one original job. Not only do you get to play sick and get paid for it, but you also test these students who are meant to be really smart and all. I bet it would feel pretty victorious if were acting as if you had one disease and the student guessed something utterly different, told you he thought you had Lyme's disease when really you were just dehydrated. Lara's explanation took up a better part of the class, so I didn't have to hear what everyone else's parents do. And I didn't have to report on mine.

THE WORLD NOT WEIGHING DOWN—SARAH

Briefly I forget who I am. This happens most often just after I've woken up from a nap. I could be anyone, or no one. I could be anywhere or kind of nowhere, in a haze. In order to wake myself up I make myself think of specific words. I think of the word livestock, or the word real estate: stock that is live, a cow you own; it is stock and alive; an estate that is real, something you can see and touch. I love the word funambulist: tightrope walker, an entertaining kind of walking. When my mother was at her lightest, when the world was not weighing down on her, she'd utter the most apt expressions that, because so accurate, were truly funny. If she was reporting on a really bad argument someone had, she'd say it was an honest to goodness knock down drag out fight. While the topic is far from funny, the expression is so exquisite, leaves an imprint on the mind.

One gesture can change everything. You think a person doesn't like you, but then, in a most unexpected moment and manner, they reach for your hand and give it a squeeze. From then on, your relation to each other is utterly transformed, never to turn back.

You can get used to anything is what I learned early on. From the thunderous to the silent, from exile to a swarming crowd. You just learn to make do. And then one day it becomes the norm. At first you feel ill at ease, but after a while the mysterious becomes as familiar as a hearthrug. One autumn, my grandfather asked me to help clear the garden spot, plant crimson clover to help the ph. level over the winter. Her said my job was to whack down the okra stalks, towering prickly hollow shafts. And for the first hour I was utterly miserable, itching all up and down my arms, scratching myself until there were welts. We took a break around 10:00 am, rinsed off in the hose. And when we got back to it, the itching was less, and I'd somehow gotten into a rhythm with it all. Of course, this is a pretty insignificant example, and happened much faster than usual, but you see what I'm after. You really can get used to anything if you have to.

SILENT MOVIES—CLARENCE

Out of the blue on Sunday, Mom announced it would be bad luck for me to enter into my teens without having ever seen a silent film. It kind of caught me off-guard but I went along with it. So, we drove to Family Video and while she looked for silent movies in the old film section, I scoured the video games. My friends are all the time talking about something they played on Wii or Xbox, and I like to be in the up and up. Mom rented Charlie Chaplin's *City Lights* and I got a box of Snowcaps, love the crunchy sound they make between my teeth. I thought I'd be full out bored by a film in black and white that has absolutely no words whatsoever. But here's the thing: even though the film is silent you kind of know what they are saying when they move their mouths. Plus, there are cards with words written on them to clue you in to what they are saying. I loved how this blind girl in the movie gets her sight back but still accepts as her friend this disheveled looking guy. Even after she sees how dirty and ripped his clothes are, she still smiles at him. She still cares for him. I told Mom I wanted to watch more silent films and she smiled. She established that as something we could do together.

Another thing from the past is typing. In school, we take keyboarding. Mom says she took typing. And boy, it must have paid off because she can write on the computer with her eyes closed. I am not kidding. She knows, in her mind, where all the keys are. One day she propped a book on the stand she sometimes uses to hold cookbooks and copied, without looking once, what the open page of the book said. I watched the whole time and could barely believe how she did it without making one single mistake. In high school her teacher covered the typewriter keys and she couldn't pass the class until she could perfectly type a page. I like watching her work on the computer. She'll be looking out the window at a bird in a tree and at the same time type a message perfectly, like a magician.

Today Mom has made it her task to continually quiz me on my social security number. Says it's something I'll need to know all the days of my life, so I might as well go ahead and memorize it right now. She has it written on a piece of paper on the refrigerator and at random times, of course when we're nowhere near the kitchen, she'll pop the question: *What's your social security number?* It kind of freaks me out, catches me off guard. So far, I've only been able to remember it once, and that was on the morning after I'd been standing at the refrigerator waiting for the ice maker to pop out another piece of ice, one of my favorite activities. I love the clunk sound it makes when the fresh, newborn piece of ice drops into the plastic reservoir.

I got a response from Peter in five days, the fastest yet:

Dear Clarence,

What great news that you are planning on taking a trip to St. Louis. There's a Waffle House two blocks from the Children's Museum, and I could meet anytime you and your mom like. When you get a chance, please give me a call so I can find out what work best with you guys. My number is 573-289-6261.

I have no plans to go anywhere until next October when I go to the Albuquerque Balloon Festival to watch hot air balloons set sail. The sky fills with over five hundred hot air balloons in every color imaginable. Some of the balloons have designs, others just brilliantly colored. You can hear the whoosh, whoosh of the pilot — that's what they call the person in charge of flying the balloon — increasing the flame so the balloon rises. It's hard to explain the majesty of this sight except to say it feels like you are in them just by watching.

Your pen pal,
Peter

INVISIBLE OR FLYING—CLARENCE

I'm glad Peter brought up hot air balloons. Sometimes in the fall one or two will be visible in the sky. All I can think of, when I see them, is how the passengers' hearts must lift the way they do on narrow bumpy roads, like your heart rises for a brief time out of where it's meant to be. Also, everything must look so small to them. Not as small as when you're in an airplane, but small enough to take out all the clutter. Also, the balloons look so silent and peaceful, but I read up on them and learned that the fire that keeps them afloat roars loudly. It gives this tremendous whoosh of fire every minute or so. I don't know why, but this all makes me think of a game I played last summer with Evan at the pool. We held our breath and ducked far under the water and pretended to pour tea for each other—an underwater tea party. We stayed at the pool's bottom as long as our lungs would allow.

How do we know what we do not know? How do we know what we know? It's like a labyrinth. You go in and in and just keep on finding out there's more to find out. When I was little, I didn't worry about this. I was constantly enthralled by new things. Like the first time I let go of a balloon, and it floated up and up and up: pure magic and delight. I didn't for one moment worry about how it happened. But now I think about what helium is and whether I can fully explain the concept of gravity and weightlessness. It's like the more you know, the more you know you don't know. I can tell you one thing: I don't know the reasoning behind some games I played when I was little. Why, for instance, do kids says *catch a tiger by his toe and if he hollers let him go* to determine who will be it in a game of tag? And who in the world came up with the game rock, paper, scissors shoot to decide who gets to go first? It's pure wildness when you really think it through.

Lately I'm troubled with the question is there a right answer. I mean, if you think about it, is there really a right—an absolutely right—answer to anything? You might say *well, of course there is.* But here's where I get myself stuck. Example: should I pick up the Styrofoam cup blowing around in the Rite Aid parking lot? At first, I think, well pick it up. It's litter. But what if, just what if, I left it and a homeless person came by and was pleased to have a cup to fill for free in the bathroom. In that case, it was the right thing not to pick it up. You see where I'm going with this.

Given the choice, invisible or flying, what would you choose? At first it seems obvious: flying. But think harder and you might see things differently. Flying has boundaries. You get to travel, yes. You can soar above the masses. You can zoom from place to place. But, at the end of the day, that's all you've done. Whereas If you are invisible, you can do and see things with no one knowing it. Wouldn't it be great to witness, unseen, what your teacher does once all the kids have left the room? Does he erase the white board? Does she dance a gig? Does the teacher just look at the room emptied of all the students? Imagine being invisible at Kroger first thing in the morning when only the manager's there. What does she do first? What if she goes over to the floral department to smell the lilies? Or behind the deli and to thinly slice herself a piece of salami so delicate it looks like a constellation of stars. These things would be possible if you were invisible. So, given the choice, mine would be invisible. I would definitely choose invisible.

If I were a tree and had a choice: deciduous or coniferous, I'm pretty sure I'd just go ahead and be a pine tree or a spruce, a conifer. It seems like a lot of work to grow new leaves each spring only to have to shed them again in the fall. Also, when the wind whips in the winter it would be far better to have some kind of needle or greenery to protect you. Don't you think?

There are two kinds of turnstiles. First, there's the kind you see on a farm which are designed to keep cows and horses in the pasture. These are made of wood and force you to walk single file through a gate in "Z" shape, something a four-legged animal could not do. Until our last trip to St. Louis, the farm kind was the only turnstile I knew existed. That's where I discovered indoor, metal turnstiles. There was one in the Children's Museum in a part I'd never explored before. Mom said they used to be all over the place. She said there was one at the Rite Aid when

Rite Aid was called People's Drug Store. She said there was one at the movie theater as well as at the craft store. They were the official entrance to places before they had computerized exit systems. These indoor turnstiles are shiny and have four arms kind of like the spokes on a bike wheel. I circled around the museum turnstile numerous times, listening to the click it made each time I took a step.

Since Peter's letter with his phone number came on a Wednesday, I had to wait until Mom got off work to tell her. As soon as she set down her keys and poured herself a bowl of cereal—she's taken to eating it after work some days, just like me—I showed her Peter's letter. As she did before, she spent a long time with it, seemed to inspect the very handwriting. But she surprised me by saying, in a casual tone of voice: *well, let's give the man a call.* Mom used her cellphone, so I couldn't hear his end of the conversation, but this is what she said: *Hello, is this Peter? This is Sarah Clark, Clarence's mom*—long pause—*yes, we were thinking of taking a day trip in the next few weeks*—another long pause—*great let me look at my calendar, if you can hold on*—pause, she goes the calendar hanging beside the fridge—*I think the 27th would be best. We'll call you once we get to the city museum and will plan to meet you afterwards. Great. Goodbye.* It was a quick call, but I shouldn't be surprised. Mom's not big about chatting away on the phone, never has been. And now it's set: trip to St. Louis, meeting Peter. I can barely believe it. It seems unbelievable. So, to seal the deal, that night I wrote him back:

Dear Peter,

Just in case Mom forgot to describe us and so you don't mix us up with other people in the St. Louis Waffle House I'm four feet eight inches tall, my hair is what people call dirty blond—a term I've always found strange cause how could a person go around with dirty hair all the time. I will be wearing a red sweatshirt and blue jeans. I'm not sure what Mom will wear, but her hair is dark brown.

Have you ever tried to make something you've seen disappear from your mind? Today it was a bird, dead on the sidewalk. It must have fallen out of its nest, was still a baby. I really wish I hadn't seen it. And just last Saturday when we went to Walmart for a poster board I needed for school I just stood there watching a kid lose two quarters on one of the claw machines that are next to the bubble gum machines right inside the door. The kid was probably six, looked like he was holding his breath the whole time that claw hovered over the stuffed animal he wanted so badly. But then the metal arm retracted, and he had nothing at all. I really, really hate that. I wish there were some way I could have helped him. I wish I had not seen it at all because I just can't get that little kid's disappointed look on his face out of my mind.

For this letter, I use a Jackie Robinson stamp. He's one of the top five people I wish I could meet. I would also like to meet Thomas Edison. How about you? What five people would you like to meet? They can be living or dead.

Clarence

WHAT DISAPPEARS IN TIME—CLARENCE

The bar of soap I use to wash my hands, the jolly rancher I'm sucking on now, the blanket I've had since I was a baby which just keeps getting smaller with each washing. Maybe that's why we hate to lose things: we know everything will eventually vanish. This disappearance is excellent news for some parts of life like the neighbor's barking dog, the substitute math teacher who thinks we still need to practice our times tables even though we had those nailed at the beginning of last year.

Five things that don't dissolve in water: oil, sand, metal, wood, and rocks. And memories, memories don't dissolve, don't disappear. Or at least some don't. And there are other things that don't even get smaller, like being afraid of the dark and wondering who your father is.

Once a week in history class, our teacher tells us we have twenty minutes to read this really long passage and then answer questions about it. Whenever we have to do this timed reading, I pretty much just seize up. The words quiver on the page, do their own little dance. I am reading about the Industrial Revolution when, apparently, the concept of home completely changed. Home went from being a place of business—you'd visit the doctor's house to get medicine, the cobbler's house to get fitted for your once-a-year pair of shoes, the milliner's house to get a hat which everyone seemed to wear all the time.

Then, boom along came the Industrial Revolution and people went to work in factories. And home became more what it is now, the place where you eat and sleep and hang out with your family. So, I am sitting there thinking about what it would be like to get a pair of shoes custom made for me when Mr. James says, *Time. Stop reading. Please answer the questions on the bubble sheet.* I know the old trick about narrowing down options until you have just two, but still, it's brutal. Why time a kid when they're doing something you've been wanting them to do all along, sit quietly and read and imagine?

In my mind, timed reading is a little bit like what happened the spring the Baltimore Orioles and the Chicago White Sox played in Baltimore, but no one was there to watch. This is because there had been riots after a guy named Freddie Gray died after the police beat him up using unnecessary force. Just imagine over 40,000 empty seats and a perfect, warm spring afternoon, but no one to eat the hot dogs or drink the beer. The news said a few fans looking in through the fence shouted Ohhh — for Orioles — at the "O" place in the National Anthem: *O say can you see by the dawn's early light.* It's hard for me to explain exactly how this is like timed reading, but they sort of live in the same place in my mind, like they have the same shape.

TREE ROOTS UNDER SOIL—SARAH

My middle school art teacher had us draw trees exclusively. All year long: trees. She said there was so much to learn from them that it was worth our while to paint and draw and charcoal and gauche and collage them. The great part was she emphasized the tree roots as much as she did the tree. Envision a calm, still lake and a tree's shadow perfectly mirrored in the water. She told us that's what a tree's roots looked like under the soil, that the roots were the mirroring of what you saw above ground. I loved thinking about that and found great comfort in having a single subject to work with for an entire year. Other kids seemed to grow weary of the tree theme. They wanted to work with cityscapes or imaginary animals. But I was content with our trees. Willows were my favorite.

TALKING DOLLS—CLARENCE

Did you know that Thomas Edison, besides inventing the lightbulb, made the first talking doll? And it was not until this year that someone figured out how to hear what those dolls said. Their sounds used to be too muffled, but modern technology allows us to hear what Edison's dolls had to say. What a thing to invent: a talking doll. When I told Mom, I'd heard this at school, she said she had a doll when she was little with red hair with a string sticking out of her back. When you pulled the string, the doll talked. There were four things she said: #1 I'm so cute #2 Do you like my freckles #3 Want to dance? and #4 Try to make me laugh. Mom explained that there was no rhyme or reason as to when she'd say which one. Sometimes her doll would repeat #2 four times in a row: *I'm so cute, I'm so cute, I'm so cute, I'm so cute.* Mom said it made her kind of ill to hear it. Next the doll would go in order 1, 2,3, 4. Creepy. I had to tell her I think the fourth recording — *Try to make me laugh* — was the creepiest of all. It makes it sound like a dare or a threat. But I can definitely see the intrigue with wanting a doll to talk.

Ever since I was little, I've found it strange how we use human words to explain what birds are saying. Usually they are made-up words like *piti-tuck* or *ri ri ro*, but others are honest to goodness words: *sally so* and *whip poor will*. And that is what I find hard to swallow. It feels like tethering down these wondrous flying beings with our own gravity to proclaim we know what they are saying. Why label their secret language with our own words? If I were a bird that would annoy me. Maybe that's why birds are outright experts at pooping on our heads and cars. It's a darn good way of getting even with us for misinterpreting what they have to say. There's even a whole category of birds called Name Sayers: Whippoorwill, Phoebe, Chuck Will's Widow, Chickadee, and Bobwhite. Who in their right mind would go around all day calling out their own name?

What's worse, much worse, is how we pretend to know why birds sing. People say birds sing to defend or gain territory or to attract a mate. I say maybe they're just singing because they can, because they like to. Maybe the bird is saying *Hey, look at that apple on the tree, it's so bright.* I get it that we want to understand and make sense of our world, but this seems going overboard. The truth is we can't really know. Maybe it would be easier to be something else other than a person. Take a fly: they live for three days, then they are done. That seems efficient to me. Or a walking stick. That's one cool presence in our world.

On the radio, there was an interview with David Allen Sibley who's written a bunch of books about birds, has a new field guide to bird behavior just out. I liked it that he said digital photography has given him access to more birds than he used to see. Before digital, people relied on actual specimens of birds. They had to use dead birds. I never would have thought of that. Not to change the subject, but I think that is one outstanding thing about the radio: how much you can find out without even trying. I mean, there you are, fixing mac and cheese with the radio on and you learn how ghost crabs walk backwards under the full moon.

SLOW MOTION—SARAH

Things make better sense when slowed down. Suddenly you can see the striped necktie on the man in back. For the first time you notice that the dog has one blue and one brown eye. You are actually able to understand what the child is asking for. I think the world just moves too fast. It's all too much. What if, for a single day, we could put all that surrounds us in slow motion? Or even for a single minute?

The philosopher Henri Bergson believed that there were two ways to measure time: real time (the time you feel, waiting for your MRI results, for a loved-one to return from a long trip) and mathematical time (what the clock says). He believed they were very different and could not be reconciled. Sometimes I wonder if the past is really the past. Over and over I think this. I'm haunted by it. If only I could stop it. It feels like a kaleidoscope, all the colors mixing without any discernible order. Am I the one supposed to make the order of it all? Being a mother requires me to have at least a semblance of order. I think we all wonder if we've made the right choices.

Here might be a place to tell you a story. After Clarence was born, I went to a healer. Instead of asking me to talk, she handed me two warm rocks, round and smooth that fit in the palm of my hand. She asked me to close my eyes, hold the stones and tell her my feelings about being a mother. I told her it felt monolithic, unwieldy, and also bright and tingly like something good and surprising could happen at any moment. Then she asked me to open my eyes. She took those stones from me and handed me two new warm stones, also smooth and perfectly sized. She said, *Now close your eyes and tell your mother's feelings about being a mother.* And here is what I said, *This is too much for me – all the responsibility, the obligation, the being tethered down. All I wanted was to be left alone to read and think and travel. Now I'm stuck, stuck forever.* Without reaction, the healer took those stones from me, handed me yet another two and said,

Tell your grandmother's story. As if I were channeling my mother's mother I replied, *I lost my figure being pregnant and now cannot get it back. It's like I've lost all control and the children are noisy and messy. My daughter is the hardest. She climbs trees and gets in the dirt. She is clumsy.*

Well, there in that healer's office, I told an entire lineage of pain, generations of it. And what came to me is that I was being given the chance to stop that cycle of seeing motherhood as a burden. From that moment on, I had been given the extraordinary chance to start afresh and enjoy this gift of Clarence.

IMAGINARY USES FOR REAL THINGS—CLARENCE

Why do drugstores sell mousetraps and wine and bird food? Seems like they should stop calling them drugstores and start calling them a-little-bit-of-everything stores or what mom says used to be called variety stores. I sometimes think about unlikely uses for actual objects. What if a fly swatter was a fan to cool off the person sitting next to you? And what if a lampshade could double as a hat? Say you quickly needed to dress up, you just grab that shade off the lamp and your outfit is complete. Or how about your snow scraper, the one you use to clear your car's windshield—what if that could be an icing spreader? You could make a bunch of cakes fast, get the cake out of the oven and then ice it likkety split.

Before there were computers, people corrected mistakes they'd made with something called white out. You can still buy the stuff—which is also called liquid paper—at CVS. I got some last winter, wanted to see what it was all about, the same way you light a match to see how it will burn even though there's no candle in sight. Well, white out is white, whiter than white, and it goes on like a kind of clumpy paint, like the finger paint we used in kindergarten. Liquid paper: talk about an ingenious invention. Mom says there were also these sheets of plastic with white on them that you'd slip in the typewriter. If you made a mistake, you'd go back over the mistyped word and the arm type hammer would slap it out white. She then gave me a mini lesson on typewriters. They are called typewriters because there are pieces of type which are these chunks of metal with raised letters on them that make perfect printed marks on the paper you have in the machine's cartridge. The raised letters are backwards, in reverse, so they print correctly on the page, the way you do a potato print.

After she explained about the typewriter, out of the blue—another phrase that mystifies me—she gave a mini speech about my Asperger's which is something she's never done before. Basically, she said that I should always be on the lookout for, and steer clear of, people who want to "fix" me. I should stay far away from anyone who says I have an "abnormality." Instead, I should try to show others that I bring a lesson to all and that if someone looks close enough, they will see me as a grouping of tiny fragments of genius. She said I could think of myself as a quilt made of precious scraps of genius and that All I can figure is that she was reading up on autism and wanted me to get the hang of what she'd learned and liked, but her mini speech felt both kind and a little scary, like she'd been worrying about me which I really hate.

Sometimes when I am getting dressed, I feel like I'm on high alert. If I wear the Cardinals shirt and they are not playing that night, or they lose, then I feel like I wore the wrong thing. I suspect we all feel this way sometimes, like it's our personal fault terrible things end up happening in the world. To make grim feelings go away, I give myself silent quizzes. Are blue popsicles sweeter than red: yes. Is seventh grade longer than sixth: yes. What kind of fishing is more challenging: lake or deep sea: don't know but will find out.

There is a man who spends his days walking the streets and alleys of Rolla wearing a reflective vest on top of a windbreaker and carrying a plastic bag from Rite Aid. He also wears two baseball caps, both blue, with an indistinguishable logo on the one he wears on top of the other. And while he looks like he doesn't think at all about what he wears, you also get the feeling he wouldn't change his getup for a million dollars— which is something he doesn't have. You see him walking about casually like this on the coldest February morning and the hottest July afternoon, always the same. Well, at least he doesn't have to worry if he wears the blue-striped shirt or the Cardinals one.

One of the additional things online are all these random quizzes: What kind of dog are you? Who were you in a past life? What does your first name say about you? Who is your spirit animal? Sometimes Mom takes these quizzes, and she seems entranced, like this is what she'd rather be doing than anything else in the world. She says it takes her out of herself, and I guess I kind of get what she means. The quizzes are tailored to help you find out who you are, what spirit animal, who's your ideal mate, what were you in a past life — but it doesn't really help you with who you are today, in the here and now, the actual living you.

In my mind, I have come up with two inventions. The first is a six-inch dip in the pavement at the end of each grocery store parking space. When you are all done shopping, you could put one wheel of your shopping cart in that hole and dip to keep the cart from running away while you loaded what you'd bought in your car. The second are rubber bumpers installed all the way around every car — like bumper cars but smaller. And they'd all be at exactly the same height on every single car. So, if you had a slight accident with another car, there would be no dents, just the bumpers bumping.

There was this guy in Italy back in the 12th century named Fibonacci who figured out that some objects have a specific, traceable pattern that can be understood with numbers. Two examples of such objects are pineapples and artichokes. Let me try to explain this phenomenon — the Fibonacci Sequence — better: the first two numbers, when added together, make the third. The second and third numbers added up make the fourth, the sum of the fourth and fifth make the sixth, and so on: 0, 1, 1, 2, 3, 5, 8, 13, 21, 34. But here's the thing, if you drew it out in tiles, it would create a spiral, like this:

and that is a shape pops up in nature all the time. Think conch shell. Think sunflower. How great that there are a series of numbers to trace those.

LOSING AND FINDING—SARAH

There are so many things we can't find a home for. Start small: the extra kitchen timer, the one you bought when you were 24 but haven't needed for years because you use your cellphone to time everything. And what about the pinch pot you made for your mother when you were in kindergarten. You kept it when you had to clean out her house after she died. What do you do with that? But there are the much bigger things that have no home. And then there are the things you have lost, permanently lost. I love Elizabeth Bishop's poem *One Art* because she talks in a light but deeply serious way about losing things, starting out with car keys, moving on to a house and ending with a lover. If you think about it long enough, losing and not finding a home have a great deal in common. It leaves this jiggly place inside you, makes you feel off kilter: a kind of vertigo of the heart.

WILL REPLACE EVEN IF LOST—CLARENCE

Peter must have written me back the very day my letter arrived. Maybe he's excited about meeting me the way I am about meeting him.

Dear Clarence,

Thank you for describing what you look like. That will help me locate you. I am medium height for an adult and am bald. I will wear a red sweater – so that will be easy to remember. Since I have no hair, when I'm outside I usually wear a hat – called a Tilly Hat – which is cream colored. I like it most because when I opened it – got it as a gift from my sister last Christmas – it came with an entire booklet full of promises: that the hat will repel the rain, that it will keep the user warm, that it has a chin strap for easy taking off and putting on. The booklet even promised – and I am not kidding – that if you lost the hat, the company would replace it for free. What if this were the case with all things in life?

I share your feelings about wanting to get certain images out of my head. It's tricky when they pop up. I have tried holding my breath – the way you do to get rid of the hiccups – to force my mind to change thoughts. And like you, I detest and dread those machines with the arms that pick up toys, only to drop them at the last minute. They seem like the exact opposite of what children should have to endure. I have an idea: let's write a letter to the editor of the St. Louis Review – I know him. We can write it together at Waffle House and tell him how we feel. Maybe he will publish it and that might make at least a few people steer their children away from them. Then, if the claw machines get little usage, maybe they will become obsolete.

You asked me what people I would like to meet. If I had to narrow it down to five, it would have to be Gandhi, The Wright Brothers, Amelia Earhart, Mary

Magdalene and my brother who died of polio before I was born. Clarence, I'm looking forward to meeting you in a little under a week.

    Your pen pal,
    Peter

FIRE DRILLS—CLARENCE

Mom says secretary is not what I should call people who help other people higher up do their jobs. The correct word is administrative assistant. This seems strange to me because secretary, as the word suggests, might involve getting to find out secrets. And isn't that something we all crave? What a cool thing to, in a course of a single day, overhear and read many things not meant for the general public. Being a secretary is not unlike being a spy.

Since we're onto the subject of secrets, I'll tell you one. I secretly love fire drills, love them at school and love them on the bus. It's like everyone goes into this different mode, quasi serious but more like acting serious than serious serious. Because we have been told to be silent and not run, it is instantly tempting to talk and run. Kids who would never dream of talking to each other at recess or in the cafeteria suddenly strike up conversations in line on the blacktop during fire drills. These two kids in my grade, Sam and Holly, avoid each other at all times. They never talk or work together—except during fire drills when they are whispering merrily the whole walk out of the building.

At the beginning of the school year, usually the second week of September, the teachers act super strict, keep on telling us to be quiet. This means the fire department is really and truly going to come, and that they will time us to see how quickly we can get out of the school building and be accounted for. In second grade, our teacher couldn't find Eddie Harper. We all stood with our toes lined up on the basketball court in silence for thirty minutes while the firemen helped the principal and vice principal scour the school. Turns out, Eddie's mom had come to get him for a dentist appointment when the class was at music, but she never signed him out. It ended up feeling scary even though there wasn't even a fire at all.

Except for that one, fire drills are great. They kill time and offer you a whole new perspective on teachers and their personalities. Most often, the ones who act all strict in class are really laid back during fire drills. Maybe the fact that they function on high alert regularly gives them the chance to let loose a bit when something official, something required by law, is asked of them. I like to watch how Mr. Herman, the keyboarding teacher, who is always super uptight in class—won't let us look at our fingers, wants us to type accurately with our eyes closed, won't let us talk, ever, during the assignments he gives us in class—strolls out for the fire drill, almost a smile on his face. One time I even spotted him talking to the cafeteria lady as if they were old friends.

On the bus, fire drills have real urgency. The bus driver gets serious. Half of us are meant to exit from the front door, the regular door, and the other half from the back door. There's also a hole in the roof, but Kevin hasn't let us climb the ladder to use that one.

It's a strange thing to do something and be timed doing it, but not have all the power over that time. If I run a sprint for a fitness test, it's up to me how long it takes, but with the fire drill it's up to all of us. You can almost feel the time ticking inside of your head: another second's passed, and another, and another. We better hurry. I feel this need to speed up much more during the bus fire drills when it's like sixty kids and only one adult.

NEGATIVE CAPABILITY—SARAH

The story I'm telling you has surely been told by countless people. Still, it feels important. I carry so much inside, so many wonderings, so many regrets, and I don't know what to do with them all. Keats' idea that intuition had dominion resonates with me. I believe in the power of the imagination much more than in reason and logic. Knowing that someone famous like Keats felt this way too helps.

When I was little, my mother hired a woman named Anna to come on Tuesday and Thursday to clean the bathrooms, iron and vacuum. Those were her supposed jobs. But the reality was that my mother left the moment Anna arrived, so I became the real job. I remember asking her to brush my hair, help me change my doll's clothing. I remember standing at her feet while she sprayed my father's shirts with starch, how the steam from the iron rose up, smelled like something not quite burnt. I knew, in the way that children just know, that Anna wanted nothing to do with me. Maybe my one clue was that she had no children of her own. She must have told me that many times. But she also just makes it clear I was an interference to her progress of getting things done. I regret, now, not trying in a different way to reach her. Why do I say this? Because I could also tell that she was very lonely and needed a friend. And maybe I could have been that friend she needed if only I'd approached it in a gentler way. But I suppose we all know that negative capability means there is something to discover, something we don't yet know. I remember learning about negative capability as an undergraduate and at first thinking it was a real thing: to be capable of nothing.

LOST CAUSES—CLARENCE

Mr. Abel told us that Saint Jude is the patron saint of lost causes. Seems like a pretty sketchy appointment. I mean, if a cause is lost, then there's little use in trying anymore, so why would you need a saint to be in charge of it? I get St. Anthony because he helps us find stuff, the watch or car key or pillbox we need or care about and really want back. But once we proclaim a cause as lost, why in the world do we need someone to oversee it? Truth be told, if I think about it deeper, further, I do understand. It's hard to let things go, just let them float away, label them lost cause. So, I'm glad there's a saint to watch over it.

I'm also glad today is free cone day at Dairy Queen. They do this once a year—think it's the company's anniversary of opening—and the cones they give are not little. They are regular sized. They'll even give you chocolate on it if you ask. I walked there after school, and sat on the bench outside eating my cone, watching all the other people who had the same idea as me.

In third grade at Wendy Simon's birthday party—had it at Wayne's Lanes—as a party favors, we got pads of special paper and three pens that wrote in invisible ink. I still have mine. Invisible ink: you can write secrets, and no one will know what you've written. Later, you take the revealer marker and go over the entire page and voila: there is what you wrote a week, a month or five years earlier. I love that. If there were a flood or a fire, I'd definitely grab my invisible ink pen and pad as one of my go-to items before grabbing anything else. No chance I'd risk losing what I'd written and thought earlier.

Most of last year there was a mouse living in my locker at school. I named him Greg and just let him hang there. I figured that was a good way for him to stay warm and safe. Because I didn't want him to eat anything I cared about, I started just using my locker to stash things like already turned in papers, old math tests—stuff like that. If I didn't eat all my lunch and if I had time, I pop on over to my locker before history — the class after lunch — and slip him some bread crust or a slice of orange. I figured it was best for me to keep Greg to myself, have him be my own private pet. I only caught glimpses of him, like the swish of his tail the minute I opened the locker, or maybe part of an ear sticking up. But there was plenty of evidence that he was there full time. If, over the week, I left a math worksheet, come Monday it would be ripped into little shreds. It made me sad when June rolled around and we all had to clean out our lockers so the janitors could sanitize them over the summer. All I can do is hope is that Greg made a beeline for a door or a hole in the wall and found himself another safe place to hang out. For all I know, maybe he's in another kid's locker this year. Maybe some sixth grader is feeding Greg saltines or cheerios. Yes, I am going to safely assume that is the case.

SOME THINGS TAKE GETTING USED TO—CLARENCE

I still don't understand what people mean when they say, *back in the day.* What I instantly think is What day? Back in what day? It's been bothering me for a really long time. Plus, whenever someone — pretty much exclusively an adult — says it, they kind of cock their head to the side like they are happily dreaming. So, I don't have it in my heart to interrupt this and question what it is they are really saying. Maybe I've just missed this one spectacular day, which is the day that everyone is referring to. My best guess is I'll never know.

And there are the other sayings that do a superb job of confusing me too. But I have figured out a few. *Long in the tooth* is one I have figured out. It has to do with horses whose teeth continue to grow throughout their lives. While ours stop sometime around 12, horses' teeth grow until the day they die. And so, their teeth get very long if they live for a while. You can tell a horse's age pretty much exactly by its teeth.

Another thing that's hard to get used to is super cold water. Mom made sure I learned how to swim when I was in first grade. So, I took lessons on Saturdays mornings at the YMCA, and what I remember most is grasping on to the edge of the pool with my face in the water blowing bubbles and learning to turn my head so that if I eventually could swim, I'd know how to take a breath. It was like learning to breathe all over again. The summer Mom and I went to Maine, I was all ready to swim in the ocean for the first time. I'd never been swimming in anything but the Y pool, so I was really pumped to try out the ocean. But the water was so cold, I couldn't even bear to walk into it. My teeth chattered the very moment I put my toe in. Mom said it takes your breath away, but you eventually get used to it. I cannot imagine ever getting used to that. Some things might just almost impossible to really get used to.

I hope that when I'm grown, I don't have hair in my nose. It seems like adults have to deal with the strangest things with their bodies, and, from what I can tell, it's not only men who have the hair in the nose problem. Clearly it would hurt to pull them out. Not something I'm looking forward to one bit. I hope I don't have to get used to that anytime soon.

I used to think sentimental value meant real money, just a kind of money I'd never heard of. To tell you the truth, it took me a really long time to realize it meant something you care a lot about, something you want to save—like a pepper grinder that was your grandmother's, the one she used when she made sausage gravy. Or a wooden nickel, a real wooden nickel, because you "won" it at the county fair when you didn't really win anything at all, but you had such a good time that day riding the Ferris wheel you know that wooden nickel will make you feel, in some small way, like you are still at the fair, smell of cotton candy and popcorn, the sticky feel of too many people all crammed together.

Larry told me today how one of the guides at Yellowstone National Park tired of tourists asking him all the time—this was before digital cameras and selfies—to take their pictures in front of Old Faithful that he started intentionally photographing just the tourists' feet. So, there they are, hoping for a stellar pic they can use as their family Christmas card, only to find out later, once they are back in the hotel or camper, that they've got a record of what shoes they wore that day. This seems mean. But I do think it would be an interesting experiment just to go out in the world and take pictures of feet.

SAY IT BACKWARDS—CLARENCE

What if we designated one day each year to say what we mean to say backwards, in reverse? You know how we have Teacher Appreciation Day, Valentine's Day, Autism Awareness Day. This year we even had Sibling Day, and everyone got to share in class something about their brothers or sisters—which left me feeling icky inside.

In fifth grade, we had spirit day and wacky tacky day and pajamas day. I'd like Say It Backwards day to be more than just in school. It would wildly change the way the world operated. Rather than saying *thank you*, you would say *you thank*. It might even be like a question *You thank?* All this has the potential to lead to a captivating interaction. Not every sentence would have to be backwards, just enough to shake things up. *Morning good. You are how? Drill Fire have we today.*

Last spring Mom and I went to a wedding—the son of a friend of hers—in St. Louis. We made a weekend out of it, stayed in a hotel with a balcony that looked down on the arch. Since I pretty much always have my binoculars with me, we could see into the little cars that carry people to the top of the arch. I could even see this one kid crying, must have been pretty scared. Mom was unwilling to go out on the balcony, but I thought that was the best part of the entire room, standing out there spying on people below. That's like saying things backwards, being so high up the world looks small.

SAYS SO RIGHT ON THE BOX—SARAH

This seems like a magnificent time to share thoughts and opinions and observation on which both Clarence and I firmly agree. Number one: the proclamations made on boxes of items you purchase should be tested. In other words, if the box says the balsam wood airplane will fly fifteen feet, and it only flies ten, we need to do something about it, preferably write the company and ask for a) a refund or b) another one that might do better. This is true with things you eat as well as those you use or wear. We do not intend to be harsh or unyielding, it's simply to have the world make sense insomuch as it can. It's like the company has made a promise with you and you're asking that they hold up their side of the deal. If everyone did this, the world might just be a little of a bit more of a fairer place.

We also agree on second chances. All living beings—people, animals, plants—should be given more than one chance to be the best they can be. If you mess up once, that is just an opportunity to learn what you did wrong. Take a geranium plant. What if you gave up on it, threw it out when some of its leaves brown? What the plant needs most at that point is for you to take off the wilted flowers, remove the not super green leaves. Then it will be the very brightest it can be. Obviously, this is true with animals, too. What if you gave away a puppy the first time it made a mistake in the house? No one would have a dog. With people the mistakes — interesting word mis take—can have higher stakes. (Notice the word stake in mistake). It seems only right to give the teenager who crashed the car, the five-year-old who bit the kid on the playground, a chance to show that's not their best selves. They simply made a mistake, like all of us do—on a pretty much daily basis.

THINGS I'LL NEVER BE—CLARENCE

To begin with, I will never ever be a PE teacher. I mean you get such a wide assortment of kids and abilities, and your job is to get everyone to move around, have fun and learn games. All that sounds okay until you take in the fact there are always a handful who have to win, no matter what the sport is—soccer, kickball, capture the flag—they are out to win, and nothing will get in their way. Put that beside the kids who don't like to exercise one bit, the ones who would far rather be playing a video game and who put about zero effort into the class. I just think it would be super frustrating. I usually just feel sorry for our PE teacher when he tries to get us all pumped up about a new activity that's sure to be a flop.

I'm also certain I'll never ever be a veterinarian. I mean, how in the world can you bear to tell someone they need to put their dog down, that their dog or cat will not live even another month, and if it does, it'll be panting in pain. It seems pretty unsettling to work on something alive that can't tell you how they feel except to squeal once the pain gets terrible.

Finally, there is no way I could ever be a fireman. I know lots of kids dream of that as a kind of heroic occupation, the enormous trucks and the triumph if it all turns out. Last August was windy and dry for the first ten days, the kind of Midwestern wind that has nothing to stop it. I was riding my bike around, seeing if I could clock six miles every day for an entire week, keeping count of it in a mini composition book I fit into my pocket. I was circling around Bear Park where there are three streets of row houses. As soon as I heard the sirens, I turned to go toward their sound. There were two huge firetrucks and more than half a dozen firemen. They looked almost to be moving in slow motion, which is the opposite of what you'd expect in such an emergency. But it got me thinking that when there's an actual emergency the people who get things done seem to be walking in quicksand, moving steadily and calmly, in slow motion.

Well, you won't believe what the firefighters did. Instead of directly dousing the two adjoining houses that had flames coming out of the second-floor windows, they aimed their hoses at the ones on either side of the fire. They literally drowned the two houses that were flank next to the burning ones. I stayed after and asked one guy, all sweating in his heavy coat and jacket, holding his helmet, why they did not directly put out the fire. He said it's the best way to safely contain a row house fire. You have to make a perimeter, so the fire won't jump and spread. Later, back at home, I researched firefighters and learned a lot about the ones who work on huge fires, forest fires. That is amazing and scary. There was a famous wildfire a long time ago in Montana called the Mann Gulch fire. Thirteen firefighters died when high winds picked up, and the fire grew super-hot and super big super-fast. Within a matter of minutes, the fire blew up and killed them just like that. It's hard to even picture it in your mind without getting sad.

Speaking of sad: Mohammad Ali died. We heard about it on the radio. The announcer said that for many years he boxed in combat boots, so when it came time for the proper match, he would feel a sense of lightness in the ring. He was really the last great heavyweight champ, such a force. It's strange how you can feel a loss even when you didn't know the person who died. There are people you never meet who have a real impact on your life. It's like they are a part of it, but apart from it. Isn't it strange how the word apart is one word, but it means separated? And if you are joined with something, say a club, you are a part of it. And those are two words. Also, a side fact: apart is a huge part of the word apartment because apartment (I looked it up) used to mean a separated place.

ST. LOUIS WAFFLE HOUSE—CLARENCE

Yesterday was remarkable. That is the best word I can think of: remarkable. We met Peter at the Waffle House near the Children's Museum at 12:00, straight up noon—which really is straight up, both hands of the clock pointing up. It's weird meeting someone you've never met because you kinda have to guess who it is based on descriptions you've pieced together. But Waffle House is a good place because you can scan the area quickly, everyone sitting down in booths or at the counter. When we saw a bald guy sitting in a booth alone, Mom and I agreed it was him. When he stood up to greet us, he was shorter than I'd imagined, not much taller than Mom, but otherwise no surprises.

We all ordered the same thing—fried eggs with hash browns—and that seemed lucky. I sat next to Mom on one side of the booth, Peter on the other. Immediately it felt like we'd known him all our lives. Maybe when you exchange letters with a person you get to know things about them that make you instant friends. But I loved meeting him in person. He spoke softly and asked us all about Rolla. He remembered everything I'd written him and referred back to my letters a lot, amazing. He seemed to really be interested in things I had told him.

But here's the thing: he brought up the mannequin topic, just like that, boom. I completely forgot to ever tell him that this was to be a secret. It wasn't as bad as you might think because he brought it up in a roundabout kind of way, said he'd just passed a store window where there were five mannequins sitting around a table looking like they were playing cards. He said it looked so realistic it made him stop. And then Mom just started talking.

To put things in perspective, Mom is not a big chit-chatter, not big on telling people things, so this was wild. Brace yourself: she told Peter about Fred. And she explained the whole thing right then and there, undid the mystery of it before my very eyes, right in the St. Louis Waffle House. What she explained is that she'd used him because she works as the night custodian at First Baptist Church and has to leave me in the apartment alone in the middle of the night while she goes and dusts and scrubs and vacuums. She sets up Fred — didn't call him that, of course, doesn't even know I've named him — in front of the gigantic front window with a book set in his lap, each night in a slightly different posture. Does this so it looks like someone's home and awake reading while she's gone from midnight to four in morning cleaning the church.

She told Peter she knows when I'm in my deepest sleep, so she doesn't disturb me by leaving and she makes sure to get home before I ever wake up. Part of me thought maybe she'd flat out forgotten I was even there. She just went on and on. Talk about getting a lot of questions answered in a bit of time! All in one fell swoop the mystery of Fred, the strangeness of the mail invoices, the reason why she takes a nap every day — all of this cleared right up. It was like an instant relief pill. Everything suddenly felt so much lighter, easier, like a weight I'd been carrying around just flew off my back.

All I can figure is Mom had been storing all this up to tell me at some point, and Peter turned out to be just the right person to spill it all to. The strange thing is, it even felt natural and okay. She slipped in that she hadn't told me earlier because she didn't want me to have to tell kids at school that my mom scrubbed toilets for a living. And that makes glorious sense. She didn't want me to get teased — given that I have plenty of other things about my life that are not exactly what you'd call mainstream. I think the best part was taking away a sense of worry I'd had. I knew — like the kind of knowing that runs past all boundaries, like a sensation, I guess is the best way to describe it — that her job at the Y was not her actual job, not her big job. For so long I had wondered why she seemed tired on a sunny day when everyone else was up and about. Her night custodian job explained all of that away.

If that weren't a big enough surprise: Mom talking nonstop, talking about Fred and her reasons for having him, she just kind of casually slipped in, slipped in like it was no big deal, that Fred had once been my dad's. She said my dad left Rolla, ran off with one of his students, when she was waiting for me to be born. The day she walked into his office to surprise him with the news of my gender, in dad's place was Fred, sitting at my dad's office desk, bent over looking like a person writing. She explained that she'd waited this long to tell me because she needed time to even out her feelings about being left like that. Mom explained that she and my dad were young and not married, but that she loved him very much. Until he ran off. Then she hated him for a long, long time. And that's why she hadn't told me about him earlier. She didn't want to tell me my dad was someone she hated. She wanted to wait until she could forgive him, or at least let go of the anger. And today, she said, she felt like she finally had. Hearing this, everything felt smooth, nothing hidden, no secrets. I felt like I could float—or better yet, fly. She said she decided not to try to find my dad or follow him. If he'd left her she wanted nothing to do with him. Having me was the greatest joy she'd ever known, she said, and she didn't need anyone to take away even a little bit of that from her.

After Mom's big talk, we stayed on at the Waffle House for a good long time, like another hour. Peter and I even wrote a first draft of a letter we'll send to grocery stores and Walmart asking them not to put claw machines in their vestibules—that's what Peter said is actually the name of the for the space between the two sets of front doors. It's a simple letter, just explains the disappointment kids feel when the arm drops the stuffed rabbit they had their hearts set on. Peter will find addresses, and then we'll both sign the letters. I've really never felt better than I did yesterday. It was like Christmas times ten. Peter said he hoped to come to Rolla in August, that we could celebrate our birthdays together. We agreed we'd meet at Waffle House again but have cake along with the breakfast. He also said he'd like to go see the world largest rocking chair, even said he'd suspend his suspicion of cars in order to go there with me. The chair is 42 feet tall and each year, on the first Saturday in August, people come from all over to get their picture taken on it. They even call it *Picture on Rocker Day*. A big truck comes to lift people up onto the seat. Of course, this is something I've always wanted to do, and now I'll get the chance. Peter and I agreed to write to each other once each week. We said it would be a way to stay connected. Mom said Peter could be like a surrogate dad, a dad who is not my dad but who does some things a dad might do.

THE MUSEUM OF THINGS THAT NEED TO CHANGE—SARAH

It is the very early beginning of spring. I can feel the lightness in my bones. And so, on my way back from First Baptist, I stop the car and watch two hot air balloons suspend in the air. How mutely they float, deeper and further into obscurity. How the passengers' hearts must lift the way they do on narrow county roads. In comparison, the train looks so small in the morning fog, and the old sycamores by the creek: they are pale as talcum. This is the world being poured into a bowl, gentle as the elephant at the zoo who maneuvers a wooden box across smooth concrete in tender starts, curious as the worlds children make, holding their breaths under water: *Eeny meeny mighty mo, catch a tiger by the toe, if he hollers let him go, my mother told me to pick the very best one and you are it.*

PANDA CAM AT THE NATIONAL ZOO—CLARENCE

We can watch, any time, day or night, this newborn panda. Her chest rises, falls, rises, falls in time with the circular chewing of her mother who absently gnaws her bamboo. I'm staring at a computer screen trespassing on lives not my own, watching them breathe and eat and sleep, watching them not know I'm watching them, these black and white bears soft as anything I can name. I wrote about them to Peter and this is what he wrote back:

Dear Clarence,

I keep on remembering snippets from our morning at The Waffle House. How delightful it was to meet you! I can tell you are one sharp cookie.

I used to live in Washington near the zoo and often visited the panda house. So, it brings me back to those days to read about your experience watching the panda cam. When I was a boy your age, I was a FONZ — which stands for Friend of The National Zoo — and I went most Sundays to check out the reptiles and also the pandas. There were two pandas named Ling Ling and Hsing Hsing. The Chinese government gave them to then-president Richard Nixon as a gesture of kindness. So, thank you for reminding me of all that. They were happy years for me.

In this package you will find a globe of the world. I thought you might enjoy having it after what you told me about your map where you mark your balloons' destinations. The reason you might enjoy having a globe is that a flat map has, by nature, some distortion. But a globe, being round accurately shows the shape and size of land and water. So, you can imagine the distance between things: one inch on the globe is right around 630 miles in actual life. I hope you find it useful and fun to have.

I am working on finding the right addresses for letters to big stores about the claw machines. Once I have enough addresses, we can get together and print out our letters and mail them. I will keep you posted.

Your friend, pen pal, and enormous fan,
Peter

When I went to pick up the package he sent from the post office—there was a note in our mailbox saying I had a package which was thrilling—the woman in front of me told the clerk she was there to pick up baby chicks, ones mailed to her from a hatchery in Iowa. When he set the box on the counter, their stalwart beaks poked through corrugated cardboard and chirping filled the room, floated over all of us waiting in line. Just like that and nothing will ever be the same.

We are studying probability in math. We had to answer questions like *If something is unlikely to happen, does this mean that it will never happen?* Took me a little to wrap my head around this whole concept, this way of thinking but once I did I liked it, way different from the regular kind of thinking we do every day. Of course, my answer to the if something is unlikely to happen does this mean it will never happen question was no. It would be great if something unlikely happened because it would define the odds. And that is what makes probability super exciting. After we answered this lengthy list of questions, they gave us a graph. The range ran from impossible to unlikely to maybe to likely to certain. We had to come up with events in our lives we thought fit in each category. Under impossible I put running a marathon in two seconds, and under certain I put that I will go to school today. I thought that was clever since I was already at school. If this were not an assignment to turn in, I would have put that I'd find out the truth about my dad on the line smack in the middle between the unlikely and impossible categories. And, lo-and-behold, now it lives in the certain category. I'm beating odds once again.

THE ART OF ESCAPE—CLARENCE

When I do something alone, sometimes I feel like I'm invisible. Let me give you an example. At Kroger, there was a cart with discounted plants: mostly shamrocks but also a few ivy plants. Well, I felt they deserved a chance, deserved a better place than a plastic cart under fluorescent lights. It was just sad how they were there, and no one wanted them. Well, I went back home, into my sock drawer, and got the two weeks' worth of allowance that were stashed there: ten dollars. And I walked on back to Kroger. With that amount I could buy four of the plants along with a snickers bar — my favorite. Now, if I suspected that anyone I knew would see me buying four shamrock plants from a rollaway cart, I probably would have thought twice about following through with my purchase, but I was lucky to have that quasi invisible feeling and so I just up and bought them. My goal is to restore them to perfect health. Plus, I think Mom will enjoy having a couple plants around the apartment. *How beautiful and irreplaceable plants are,* she once said. And I agree.

I get the feeling that birds think of themselves as invisible. How else would they be willing to poop on people's cars and heads? There's no way you'd do that if you thought someone could identify you as the culprit. Plus, birds really are amazing — inhabiting two worlds at once. In college, Mom took a bunch of classes about birds — ornithology classes. And sometimes she slips in facts she knows when we're out driving or at Bear Park. Yesterday I told her I think seagulls look like hotdogs with wings. She agreed and said so do chimney swifts. Two amazing bird facts she's told me over the years: purple martins can sleep while they are flying. And hummingbirds can too. How else would they make it all the way across the ocean when they migrate each year? There are certain things you cannot un-think, like I've said before. And flying while asleep is certainly on that list. Sometimes I say to myself: Take a step back. What is it you see? Today it's hummingbirds flying—zoom so fast.

THE ART OF ESCAPE—SARAH

Remember how Beethoven wept after performing the ninth symphony for the first time? By then he was completely deaf. What he felt we will never know. All those hands clapping must have created a tremendous vibration. Was he distraught because he couldn't hear? Or was he so astounded by what he'd just done? More often than we allow ourselves crying is the right reaction. This story, I expect, sticks with lots of us. It's like, in his deafness, he was encased in a bubble and the clapping touched the perimeter of that bubble, allowing him the possibility of escape. I keep coming back to this in my mind.

Yesterday I was going through Clarence's school papers from fifth grade and came upon one which much have been from math as the focus was probability. On the worksheet, he was asked the question: *If something is unlikely to happen, does this mean that it will never happen?* His answer: *no.* Next, the question: *If something is likely to happen, does this meant that it will always happen?* Clarence: *no.* On the other side of the sheet there was an exercise in which he had to rate events on a scale of likelihood: impossible, unlikely, maybe, likely, certain. Under impossible he wrote: *Jumping across the Grand Canyon with no help.* Under unlikely: *that it will snow and cancel school.* Under maybe: *finding out who my dad is.* How much we find out by looking at work done in private.

After he gets home, he suggests we go on an outing, a walk, to Bear Park. I think he is practicing what he might show Peter when he comes tomorrow. We walk to the wooded part on a worn, trail and it feels like we are barely moving, like we are swimming, somehow, with the tall grasses beside us. Then, amazingly, Clarence takes my hand. I feel it as a brush, first, but then a real grip. He pulls and we both begin walking faster. We are walking in step with each other holding hands.

ENDLESS POSSIBILITIES—CLARENCE

We learned in social studies that some Buddhists believe there are fourteen questions you shouldn't even try to answer. You must leave those question be, let them float, remain unknowable. They are questions like *Is the world eternal? What was I in the past? What will I be in the future?* The Buddha flat out refused to answer any of these questions, our teacher explained, because he didn't want to think about things that were unreal. He said it would trap us into thinking of the past and the future when what we should really be thinking about is the present.

So, I made up my own list. Here are a few: Why does time exist? Why are moths drawn to light? Why do you yawn if someone near you does? There are more growing in my mind, but I haven't fully formed them yet. Maybe more important than these questions, though, is one answer I have come up with: effort matters. The attention and thought a person puts into what they choose to do counts a lot. Let's picture the Statue of Liberty. It stands at 151 feet one inch tall. The dude who designed it and those who helped him put such care into their work, they even used gold leaf on the torch. They meticulously sculpted Lady Liberty's head and crown. But take a moment just to think this one through: they did all this 17 years before the Wright Brothers even figured out how to fly. So those who built the Statue of Liberty put precision into something that they must have believed would never be seen close up. Still, they put the greatest care into what they did. People just don't do that much anymore.

It's early spring now, and leaf helicopters all whirling off the oak tree across the street. I like to stand under them and make it in my mind that it's raining, but with no water, no need for a coat or umbrella. For reasons I cannot say, it reminds me of the way the apartment shakes when the train goes by, clip, clack, clip, clip. Today Peter's coming to Rolla, and I will take him to Bear Park. I feel like someone just invented the telescope and there are a million places to look, endless possibilities that only now we can see.

LETTER TO CLARENCE—SARAH

I write this letter to Clarence hoping someday I may find it in me to give it to him. Not yet. I can't do it yet. I'll keep it in my dresser. But here is what I want to say to him.

Dear Clarence,

I used to spend afternoons mending books that kids had swashed around in their backpacks. It was one of my first jobs, the only one I've ever had where I was certain I was causing no harm. I was fixing something, mending books. That's what I really want to say to you, Clarence: try to find a way to repair things in this life. It actually feels like book mending to even write this letter. Maybe it will be a way to repair what has come apart between us.

Because distrust was my mother's constant companion, because she wanted me to know this in a way that would make my teeth ache, that's the last thing I want to pass on to you. When I was about your age, I saved up my allowance to buy iron-ons of ladybugs to decorate my favorite pair of jeans. As soon as my mother spotted them, she turned away, announced that they would just come off in the first wash. She even distrusted iron-ons.

I believe there are variations on the truth. And there are countless ways to tell a story.

Take Hansel and Gretel, which I think of a lot. In one version, there is a lake the children need to cross over after escaping the witch's house, and they employ a white duckling to ferry them across. In another version, there is neither a lake nor a duck. And Cinderella: in Thailand, her dead mother comes back in the form of a fish that Cinderella talks to for comfort when things get rough with the wicked stepmother. The fish even ends up protecting Cinderella in hazardous situations. It whisks her up on its tail fin to keep her from getting burned when she's cleaning out a fireplace whose coals are still red hot. In Greece, in place of a fairy godmother who helps her go to the Royal ball, there is Mother Nature who gives Cinderella – who is simply called the orphan – radiance from the sun, warmth from the moon, grace from the dawn and blue shoes from the sea. That one is so lovely, far better than a prince charming and a glass slipper which can – and inevitably will – shatter into hundreds of perilous shards.

And there are real and interesting reasons to tell stories. They can make the truth, at least temporarily, bearable. This is why I did not tell you that your father left Rolla the minute I told him I was pregnant with you. That's what he did. He left. And I can't find it in me to tell you that. To say it out loud. I want to create for you a protective coating, the kind beetles have, so you won't get stung or nicked by life as you meander through it.

You have a gift, Clarence. You notice things that the rest of us ignore. Yesterday you and Peaches were sitting by the window and you gasped when a truck pulled in and scared all the birds off. You felt their displacement viscerally. I wish I could help you make sense of all you hear and see and feel so deeply.

So, I try to hold fast to the good parts. You've told me your favorite thing about school is the question of the day. I remember the day you said, Mom, get this: there can be as many right answers as there are kids in the room. And I could tell by your tone of voice that you just love it. I'm thinking this question of the day is like Cracker Jack Prizes when I was a kid. Inside that box of sweet caramel and popcorn, inside something already great, would be a plastic whistle or a miniature car or a spinning top. One time I even got a perfectly functional three-inch kaleidoscope. I kept it in my backpack for weeks, maybe even months. But what if the Cracker Jack box advertised the fact that it came with a top? What if the box said there was a kaleidoscope inside? That would not be nearly as wondrous as being surprised by the treat, as opening the little wrapper and finding that top or a bright kaleidoscope. The surprise is in some ways the most magnificent part. And when you think of it, when someone cares enough to ask you a question, cares enough to really and truly listen to your answer, that is caramel. And if we deem all answers good, that is a surprise toy, a veritable treasure.

When I was your age, we'd play rock paper scissors shoot whenever a choice had to be made: who gets the last popsicle, who gets the swing without the mud puddle, who rides shotgun. It seems a fair enough way to suss out these sorts of situations. That being said, I doubt if fairness is a quality we should put *much stock in or even realistically hope for. Life is, by nature, unfair—plain and simple. And things go a lot better if we learn early on to get used to that fact. I'm sorry I haven't yet had the heart to explain this to you or to tell you of the other things I am keeping secret. I'm just not yet ready to say, Clarence, life is not fair. And that's just the way it is. Get used to it now while you are young. I just haven't had the heart to break it to you. At least not yet.*

Love, Mom

When faced with tricky decisions, I remember how in high school two friends and I set out to read Dante's Inferno, cover to cover. We made a club of the entire thing, meeting in basements, unpacking the scenes, reading passages aloud. And even though I was, at times, outraged by all the hardships the characters had to go through, by all that darkness and strife, what I found exquisite was Dante's belief that there is an actual place called Dis which was filled with shadow and uncertainty, mystery really. Dis is where nothing is all the way clear or knowable. Think foggy mountain pass where suddenly you can barely see your hand in front of your face.

As humans, we categorize the "dis" words—disjunction, disability, disquieting, disarming—negatively: no function, no ability, no quiet, no protection, if you think about the history of dis you find it to mean apart or in a different direction. It can also mean asunder. Let's just take two of the words: disease and disaster. Disease means ease gone asunder. Disaster means an ominous alignment of the stars, stars arranged unfavorably. It does not mean no stars.

I've grown used to the fact that there are plenty of things I cannot find an answer for. There are the small unknowables like why construction paper comes in packs of 48, not 50. And at the movie theater, which armrest is yours? But most often it's what I have done that stumps me. I look back on decisions I have made and ask myself what in the world I was thinking. I have no answer to explain why I stayed here in this midwestern town after Henry left. This is a tiny place with so few jobs, so little for me to do. I knew I'd end up having to piece things together, take a bunch of odd jobs—like cleaning a church—to pay the bills. Maybe I stayed because it's a safe and behind-the-times kind of place, wide front lawns and not much crime, not much at all going on. I love the fact that there's still a store called Family Video where you can rent movies for a dollar. And how, if you are here long enough, you know everyone, and everyone knows you. I find comfort by all the predictability. And I can attest to the fact that the people here are kind and real. What you see is what you get. And we all know that's not the case in much of the world.

TAKE A PICTURE OF YOU TAKING A PICTURE OF ME— CLARENCE

Did you know that a propeller on an airplane spins so fast that in a photograph it looks still, appears to not be moving one bit? How strange is that, that something moves so fast that its motion can neither be caught nor recorded? At school my elective is photography. Last week the teacher let us wander around the building—only inside—and take pictures of whatever caught our eye. Evan and I cruised around together. We took some shots of the tile designs in the cafeteria and some overhead lights in the library. We were trying to capture the lights' annoying buzzing sound, but there was really no way to get that on film. For the last ten minutes, we just took pictures of each other taking pictures. Evan started it by suggesting, *I'll take a picture of you taking a picture of me.* It was dizzying in a way to think about it, like thinking about thinking. Have you ever done that?

Mom's got a calendar in a box, that's the best way to describe it. It's a plastic box with faded letters that reads *Turn your dial to WVOL.* There's a button on top of the box, and when you press it, a metal flag comes down and the date moves, changes from the 11th to the 12th or the 22nd to the 23rd. In a little slit are the months of the year written on miniature metal pieces. When one month is over, you slip in the next month for display. Mom said the radio stations used to give these calendars away when she was a kid. I love hearing each morning when Mom clicks the number to the next day. It makes the new day official. It makes it so we can start all over, a fresh new day. It is a miracle, veiled and out of sight, utterly full of hope.

NOTE FROM THE AUTHOR

Word-of-mouth is crucial for any author to succeed. If you enjoyed *The Collapsible Mannequin,* please leave a review online—anywhere you are able. Even if it's just a sentence or two. It would make all the difference and would be very much appreciated.

Thanks!
Charlotte

ABOUT THE AUTHOR

Charlotte Matthews' published works include a memoir, *Comes with Furniture and People* (Black Rose Writing) and three poetry collections. Her work has appeared in *Rattle*, *The American Poetry Review* and *The Journal of American Medicine*. Recipient of The Adele F. Robertson Award for Excellence in Teaching, she has received fellowships from The Chautauqua Institute, The Virginia Foundation for the Humanities, and The Klingenstein Foundation. She is Associate Professor at The University of Virginia.

Thank you so much for reading one of **Charlotte Matthews'** novels. If you enjoyed the experience, please check out our recommended title for your next great read!

Comes with Furniture and People by Charlotte Matthews

2020 Next Generation Indie Book Award Finalist - Women's Issues

View other Black Rose Writing titles at www.blackrosewriting.com/books and use promo code **PRINT** to receive a **20% discount** when purchasing.

CPSIA information can be obtained
at www.ICGtesting.com
Printed in the USA
LVHW010108090121
676100LV00002B/329